WHAT THE FAMILY NEEDED

Steven Amsterdam was born in New York and has worked as a map editor, producer's assistant, and a pastry chef. He has lived in Melbourne, Australia since 2003, where he works as a writer and palliative care nurse. His debut novel, *Things We Didn't See Coming*, won *The Age* Book of the Year in Australia and was longlisted for the *Guardian* First Book Award.

ALSO BY STEVEN AMSTERDAM

Things We Didn't See Coming

STEVEN AMSTERDAM

What The Family Needed

VINTAGE BOOKS
London

Published by Vintage 2013

2 4 6 8 10 9 7 5 3 1

First published in Australia in 2011 by Sleepers Publishing,
Melbourne

First published in Great Britain in 2012 by
Harvill Secker

Vintage
Random House, 20 Vauxhall Bridge Road,
London SW1V 2SA

www.vintage-books.co.uk

Addresses for companies within The Random House Group Limited
can be found at: www.randomhouse.co.uk/offices.htm

The Random House Group Limited Reg. No. 954009

A CIP catalogue record for this book
is available from the British Library

ISBN 9780099565932

The Random House Group Limited supports the Forest Stewardship
Council® (FSC®), the leading international forest-certification
organisation. Our books carrying the FSC label are printed on FSC®-
certified paper. FSC is the only forest-certification scheme supported
by the leading environmental organisations, including Greenpeace.
Our paper procurement policy can be found at:
www.randomhouse.co.uk/environment

Printed and bound by CPI Group (UK) Ltd, Croydon, CR0 4YY

What the Family Needed

Giordana

At last, they were arriving in the land of normalcy: streetlamps, parked cars, and hedges. And there was Alek, holding onto a full glass of milk and spinning circles in the middle of a moonlit lawn.

Giordana had to at least be thankful her mother wasn't checking them into a motel this time.

The blue hatchback swerved into the driveway, messing up the gravel and ending Alek's little dream. A pile of clothes and books that had divided the back seat between Giordana and her brother Ben finally fell across her lap.

She watched Alek run across the grass, up the front steps, call inside, then race to the head of the driveway. Gleeful in their headlights, he hopped up and down in a welcome dance, miraculously never spilling the milk. He waved the glass over his head, toasting their arrival.

Over the sound of her mother's last-minute instructions and her brother's resolute humming to his headphones, Giordana heard Alek call out, "Greetings, cousins!" He would make this bearable. His Superman underpants stuck out from his jeans. "They're here!" he shouted at the house.

Giordana unpacked herself from the clothing and sheets and kitchen crap that jammed the car to capacity, and climbed out into the still, chirping, suburban air. When he was good and ready, Ben got out too. They watched their mother paw through the junk to see what she wanted to bring inside first.

Giordana collected the facts. One: her parents had had an argument. A shocker. Two: once again, Dad was left in a cramped apartment on a street with trucks rolling by in the morning and rats creeping by at night. Three: the plan was that the family, minus Dad, was going to camp out at Aunt Natalie's till it all went away. Right. Giordana stayed close to the car.

Aunt Natalie's was the kind of house you would draw with a crayon if you had just learned squares and triangles. It would be home for the next week or two.

Ben was yawning as if nothing mattered. Since he'd turned seventeen and started staying out all night, she knew that if she didn't watch him every minute he could walk off and start living his life without them. A mere twenty months younger, she wasn't going to let herself be left behind. But anything was possible. After all, a woman had written a note to her husband and driven away with their kids. Tomorrow, Ben might decide it was his turn to make a sudden exit. Their mother might decide she didn't want to be a mother anymore. Anyone could leave anyone. Giordana couldn't think about it.

Aunt Natalie and Uncle Peter finally came out to the front step and beckoned them towards the front door.

Peter called, "You can unpack later. Come."

Giordana gave Ben's hair a tug to mobilise him. He said, "ow" loudly enough to draw attention to her, but she didn't care because she was the one being mature, trying to get him inside. Each of them was loaded up with a duffel bag and a pillow and pushed towards the house.

The better memories of her father, which seemed to be taking up space in exactly nobody's mind but hers, would have to be put on ice for a while. Going up and saying hello was what the situation demanded. Giordana dragged Ben along.

Giordana's mother had a successful double in life and it was Aunt Natalie. She was even more serene tonight than ever, as if she fed off her sister's disasters. She was all mellowness, wearing tan pants and an unwrinkled olive shirt, like she had been at the piano practising Bach when they drove up. Beside her on the bench would have been chamomile tea in a flowered cup. Always just so. Natalie stood on the threshold and spread her arms wide for a hug.

"Oh Ruth," she said, pulling the three of them into the hall. "I am sorry. It's rotten."

"It is. It really is," Giordana's mother said, stroking her children with pity that she mainly had for herself.

Uncle Peter provided the male version of the same warm hug, patting everyone's back once or twice. He said, "You know you're free to stay as long as you need, if not longer."

For most of the three-hour runaway drive, Giordana had begged her mother to turn back. Now, she was glad they were all crushed together under the hallway light.

Alek squirmed in and asked his mother, "Can I take them on the tour?"

Natalie shushed. "This is a difficult time. They don't feel like playing."

Alek was still bouncing. "Why not? We're all together. That's what's important, right?"

"Please wait," said Natalie, not loosening her hold on the three of them. The embrace was a treatment and she hadn't finished applying it yet. Behind her, a corridor of framed family photos held out the promise of stability and happy memories in the future. Off in the front room, Giordana saw the whole TV corner. Picture it: a family sitting around, watching movies together. A quiet night with popcorn and no doors slamming. See what the right father and a little money in the bank could produce?

Uncle Peter said, "Your choices are the study next to the boys' room that has an old chaise longue, or there's the big pullout sofa downstairs. Who values privacy more than comfort?"

"Me," said Ben, with first-born authority. His decision was ratified without debate. So Giordana would cuddle up with her mother. To be expected.

Alek wrapped his fingers around his cousins' wrists to pry them away from the huddle, "Let me take you on the tour now?"

Ben told him, "We took the tour last time. Remember?"

"Then I'll change it!"

"Sweetheart," Natalie said.

Given the choice, Giordana would have preferred to stay with her mother and hear how she would tell the story of leaving. It would all be said differently if Giordana weren't in the room, though. How would Natalie and Peter react? Would her mother see their pity? The responsible thing to do was to go play with her cousins.

Giordana fluttered her hand at her face like it was a royal fan and told Alek, "A tour would be divine!"

Alek focused on her. "Okay, tell me which you want: to be able to fly or be invisible?"

"Is this part of the tour?"

"Which do you want? Whatever pops into your head first. Just say it."

"Can I walk through things or do I have to slip in and out of rooms when the door is open?"

Alek thought it over. "No. Okay, yes, you can go through walls. But you can't steal stuff, like from the bank."

"That's all right. I'll restrain myself. Invisible."

She gave Ben a glare to make him accompany them. Ben bent his elbows up and waved his hands sarcastically at his sides. "In that case, I'll fly."

Alek was satisfied. "Good. Follow me."

The tour led directly upstairs to the boys' bedroom, no surprise. Sasha was on the upper bunk, reading under a teal blanket.

"Sasha's going through a shy period," Alek announced.

Sasha threw the covers back to shout, "Am not!" and went back to his book.

Having the audience of real teenagers, it was easy for Alek to ignore his older brother. In the middle of the room, Alek stopped the tour to study Giordana's face.

Giordana opened her mouth to ask why, but he silenced her. "I'm pondering," he said.

Inspiration came. From a dozen plastic animals and monsters marching across a dresser, he retrieved a Godzilla and put it in her hand. "Here."

With that formality out of the way, he got down to the business of pulling games off a shelf and spilling them onto the carpet.

Giordana followed Ben's gaze out the window to the street below. A girl around Giordana's age was biking in bored infinites in the middle of the intersection. No cars around, so why not? At night here, a boy could spin on a front lawn and a girl could bike in the street. This place was that safe.

The rug had a rainforest design on it and Alek spread out over the treetop-and-monkey part. The game boards were aligned so that their corners touched in a triangle.

Alek began spouting made-up rules for a whole new game that no one could follow.

"You're going to get the pieces all mixed up," Sasha said, from a crack in his covers.

Alek said, "You're not playing."

If anyone was going to rein Alek in, it would have been Giordana, but she was distracted by the sound of someone sliding a window open across the street. It was that quiet, too. People liked the leafy streets for a reason, she was sure, but this wasn't her. This was not the summer she had planned. Until she was back with her friends, she would be marked absent from life.

School had ended three days ago. She had lined up a part-time job scooping ice-cream at Sprinkles four times a week. The job was totally lame, but it came with free ice-creams whenever the manager was out. Furthermore, Thea's parents had left her alone for a week and their apartment was going to be a base of operations for sleepovers where no one would sleep, where the blender would be full of rum and fruit juice, and where the mornings would be dominated by fashion extravaganzas, exclusively sponsored by Thea's mother. These things were facts that no longer mattered. Because now, at the same time that all of her friends were together, Giordana was standing there in Alek and Sasha's bedroom. Total weakness.

Invisibility would have been a relief. Not having to be seen by anyone as she limped through a dull week or two of suburban solitude. She could eavesdrop on her mother as she patched things up with her father and hear what new short-term fixes they were putting on their marriage. What was the bare minimum her father would have to say this time? She knew most of her parents' secrets because their conversations usually happened at top volume. But if she were out of sight, she could listen to other people too. What did a regular girl say to a regular boy?

As she was thinking about walking in a park and over-hearing some dreamy-dippy lovebirds cooing, Ben called her name. He looked around the room – right at her, prac-tically – then stuck his head into the hallway and called out, "Giordana, where the hell are you?" He looked back into the room, at Alek. "Where'd she go?"

Alek glanced up, but then went right on jumping pieces around the game boards. He didn't see her either.

She looked down at her hand and saw nothing, only the floor beneath her.

What Giordana didn't say was, "I'm right here."

Instead, in two backwards steps, she withdrew from the centre of the room, staying quiet and close to the wall. There was a creak or two, but nobody looked in her direc-tion. Ben called her name again. Hanging on the far wall, there was a wooden boat with a triangle mirror in its sail. Giordana swivelled to look at herself and saw only the wall behind her. Her face flushed, but she couldn't see it. She was gone.

From his bed, Sasha was watching the chaos Alek was making with disapproval. Giordana waved her arm in front of him. He didn't see her either.

Ben shouted out into the hall, "Oh great, you drag me up here and then leave me here with this nut." When he didn't get a response, he kneeled down next to Alek, letting him know it was the biggest favour in the world. "All right kid, tell me how we play this game of yours."

Giordana took an alley cat step into the corner of the room, between the bunk bed and the wall. She put the Godzilla model down on the dresser. As she let go of it, it became visible. When she picked it up again, it disappeared. She let it go and it appeared.

All right then.

Steering clear of Ben and Alek and all the game pieces, Giordana left the bedroom. In the hallway, she padded softly along the corners of the floorboards to keep them still. Wait: if her feet were causing the creaks on the floor, then she must have body mass. She stopped and tried pressing her forehead against the wall. Her head didn't proceed through it. A barrier. Stuck in this deadlock with the plaster, she stared at the wallpaper. Rose bushes and gardening tools, a sweet shorthand for a happy household. The reds were like fire engines. Uncle Peter probably dusted the walls twice a month. Giordana kept her breathing steady, concentrating and pushing her head harder. No matter how she focused, she couldn't advance through. Her father's permanent sense of outrage surged inside, demanding she go back and make Alek tell her exactly how to walk through walls. *If he gave you this goddamn ability, it had better work two hundred per cent.* But this wasn't a toaster you could throw at the woman at customer service.

Besides, it wasn't Alek's trick. She had simply never tried before. With some practice, she would figure it out.

Giordana went into the bathroom. There was enough light coming in from the moon. In the mirror over the sink, she saw the reflection of the shower curtain behind her. No Giordana. Invisible. What if this was forever? Life as she knew it, ended. She thought about her face, how her father had once told her she smiled with her eyes and should try doing it more often. She tried smiling consciously for the mirror. Her features, her body came into view. *Thank you, whoever you are,* she thought. As good as it would have been to disappear from surface life for a while, permanent invisibility would have created logistical problems. She imagined her own nothingness again and watched herself dissolve in the mirror. This was incredibly excellent.

Downstairs, she followed the sound of her mother's monologue to the airconditioned kitchen. Peter was pouring coffee. Natalie was putting away dishes.

Giordana stood in the doorway. They didn't see her.

Her mother said, "He knew we were going. He knew. He didn't come home tonight to a shock. The first time Ben got drunk was the clincher. I wasn't going to wait around to watch that develop. The boy lacks enough motivation as it is."

Giordana couldn't agree more.

Peter held out a packet of vanilla creams. "Ruth?"

She gave a no-thanks wave. After all, if her mouth were full she wouldn't be able to talk.

Giordana wanted one though, and started angling to see how far she could go into the room without being observed.

Her mother went on. "I can't believe it's finally real."

The best strategy was to let her mother tell and retell the story till it was all used up. Natalie must have sorted that out a long time ago, because she didn't try to say anything.

Giordana stood an arm's-length away from a biscuit. All Peter had to do was stop eating them and put the packet down. As soon as she touched one, it would vanish and be hers. Would they hear her chewing?

Her mother's talking provided cover for the operation. "I kept waiting for him to screw up and, boy, he kept not letting me down."

Natalie squared the packet so that the edge lined up with the counter-top. Giordana took a step closer.

"When he quit that last job – some new pointless rage, everyone else's fault but his own – he came home and started fuelling up that anger. No way I was still going to care."

She had told Giordana he was fired.

"It was smart of you to wait for the end of the semester," Peter said.

"Oh no, I couldn't have torn them away any earlier. Besides, I had to plan."

Hold it: in the car, Giordana consoled herself that this was another of their marital 'hiccups', as her mother had renamed a previous drama. Was sharing a pullout sofa part of a plan?

"It's bad enough I'm uprooting them. But they'll make it. Ben could do with finding some different friends. And Lord knows Giordana will survive. You've seen her; she stays calm like I never could. She's the oldest of souls."

The oldest of souls.

Giordana was picturing each of those words when Peter reached for the biscuits and his hand brushed hers. He twitched when their skin touched, but Giordana let go quickly, leaving him in control of the pack again. All right, she definitely had mass. With two silent steps she retreated from the risky middle of the room.

The sound of the front door opening. Who left it unlocked?

It was the girl who'd been biking in circles, letting herself into the house.

Giordana struggled to wrap her mind around everything. One: the fact that all of this was planned. Why hadn't she been told? Two: her mother's mystical praise. Was thinking that Giordana possessed superhuman wisdom easier than giving her any serious consideration?

Three: now this girl. Who was she? Definitely not an in-between fifteen. She was a little older, with actual breasts. She had hyper-conscious hair and skin. It was a defensive observation, but still: the serene pretty face and the shining brown wisps required time that could only be evidence of character flaws. If they were at the same school, she surely would have been at least one or two tiers above Giordana. They would never have a reason to speak.

"Hello-oo?" the girl called from the hall.

Uncle Peter lurched from the kitchen, "We're in here." Giordana missed her opportunity to snag a vanilla cream, only managing to scurry out of the way as the girl strode past her into the kitchen – so close that Giordana copped a blast of Calvin Klein's Obsession. Like she owned the place, the girl pulled the swinging door shut after her and lectured about conserving electricity.

Giordana couldn't pass through the door, but she could hear Natalie's introductions.

"Janelle, this is my sister Ruth. She's visiting with her kids for a while. Janelle usually babysits for the boys, but she's working at a children's camp this summer."

Her mother had been introduced as the sister. No mention of separation, divorce, abandonment.

Uncle Peter said, "You must be about Giordana's age."

"I'm sixteen," Janelle said.

Ruth helpfully pointed out, "Giordana's fifteen."

Camp leader, whatever that meant. A bit more interesting than scooping ice-cream. Probably more money, too. And though she was the babysitter, she had come over to visit Peter and Natalie as if they were friends.

"Coffee?" Peter asked her.

"Sure, Peter. Thanks."

Sure, Peter. Coffee. Giordana was outraged on so many different levels that she didn't know where to start. Were they going to jazz it up with a shot of whisky like her father did?

Her mother volunteered that since Janelle was busy with camp, Giordana would be free for babysitting while they were staying.

Peter said, "We'll pay the going rate."

"Don't be ridiculous," her mother said, as if money didn't matter at all. She pushed the kitchen door open, practically into Giordana's forehead, and shouted, "Giordana, come down!"

Right, she was still upstairs.

Giordana went to the hall bathroom so she could supervise her reappearance in the mirror. There she was again. Her face wasn't bad – nothing canine, but not exactly feline either. One long moment was allowed to pass so a smile could rise before she had to make her entrance – the way Thea had advised her to adjust herself before answering the phone. It made her voice friendlier, she said. Thea's mother had a subscription to *Cosmopolitan*.

Having seen and smelled Janelle already, Giordana entered the kitchen with something she didn't like to think of as an upper hand, but which was, at best, a minor upper hand.

Introductions were done. The girls gave each other warm hellos, but those were cheap.

No one offered Giordana coffee.

Janelle was holding court in the middle of the room, talking about the kids on her camp and turning her cup around on the counter.

Peter leaned against the sink, and – Giordana was certain – paid close attention to Janelle's movements. It was a little obvious, sleeping with the babysitter. Surely Natalie would have noticed. But maybe marriage numbs things. Giordana thought of her mother. Maybe it made you switch off a little so you could get on with your own life. Or maybe it made you switch off everything.

Janelle volunteered the use of a spare bike while Giordana was visiting. And, since Janelle had the next two days free, she could show her around the neighbourhood. Giordana, who had nothing to offer in return, said okay, and admitted to herself that she would be glad of the company. Besides, if Janelle was screwing Uncle Peter, this would be the way to obtain proof. Giordana wasn't sure if she was more disgusted with Peter for being weak or Janelle for being evil. Or was it the other way around?

Ben came into the kitchen, with Alek and Sasha right

behind him, all of them demanding biscuits. Ben gave Janelle a non-committal "hey". Alek gave her a high-five, timed with a man-sized burp.

"Alek," Peter said.

Alek replied with the same impatience. "Dad."

Janelle didn't distract easily, and continued talking to Giordana, "Is eight-thirty too early? I'm still stuck on my school wake-up time."

Giordana, who had thought she would be spending the next few weeks alone on her aunt's verandah reading, said "cool" before she could even remember how much she hated the word.

"There are definite, long-term details that you know about people, that you've always known about people in your life from very early on. You keep them in separate drawers from the daily-use details." Her mother was trying to explain away their departure while developing a system for the bags of clothing spread out on the floor. Giordana took her time to make up the sofa bed, so that she wouldn't be asked to do more than that.

Her mother continued, "You block them out because you can't even imagine that they're important or you don't think a time will ever come when you have to face them." She was working hard on this one. "You expect that the problems in the bottom drawer or in the back of the wardrobe or wherever you've hidden them will stay there forever. That they won't ever apply to you."

"Like our winter coats that we left with Dad?"

"Like Dad," her mother said.

"That's lame. Dad's not a detail."

"You're right," she said, and gave Giordana a pat on the head. She started to refold the contents of one bag so that it would at least prop up neatly on the floor. Giordana watched her, irritated. They hadn't packed, they had evacuated. None of this was necessary. If Giordana had been given some warning, she could have planned, could have said goodbye to her friends.

In school they had talked about displaced populations and she wondered if this was, on an infinitesimal scale, what that felt like – being washed out of one home and forced to find a new one. Misplaced was different. That was when you were lifted entirely out of the picture, lost. She was displaced. Dad was misplaced.

With a noisy sigh, her mother got to her knees to sort the boots and belts that didn't fit into sensible piles. "I know you're at a vulnerable age, darling, but I swear to you, as soon as we get settled some place, we'll get you therapy."

Giordana didn't want therapy. She wanted a home. This wasn't it; their last apartment (where her father was probably drinking himself to sleep) wasn't it. Giordana looked at her fingers as she shoved the pillows into their cases. A sentence came to her that could have been in an old advertisement: *Knobby knuckles, not so nice.* She already knew she would never be a hand model, or any kind of model, really. If Natalie had been her mother, her hands would be beautiful and she and Janelle would have been friends for fifteen years.

Her mother wasn't looking at her. This would be a good time for a dry run. Giordana tried to space out on nothingness, clearing her body of visible particles. She looked around. She was still there, hands and all. Again, she tried. Again, nothing happened.

It had all been mental. A shock response to leaving so suddenly. People's hair turned white sometimes in times of crisis.

Extreme disappointment, not to mention the so-very-pathetic reality of sharing a bed with her mother, circled in. Her brain had given her a flashy hallucination and then taken it away. It disappeared – how ironic. Still, it was better that she found out the whole thing was a fantasy this way than if she had idiotically started bragging to Janelle, *Look what I can do!*

Practice and more concentration were needed. Dutifully, she went back to the bathroom to try one more time. She stood in front of the mirror and slowly considered herself entirely there but entirely gone. She was relieved to see she was still able to think herself away. Holding onto the thought like a too-full bowl of soup, she walked back to the living room. Her mother had pushed their belongings between the metal legs of the sofa bed. There they wouldn't disturb the clean lines of Aunt Natalie's happy home.

"Um?" Giordana said.

"Yes?" Ruth said, not turning around.

"I've got a question," waiting for her mother's gaze.

"And your question is…?"

Giordana stayed silent. As Ruth sat back on the floor to face her daughter with full attention, Giordana felt herself become visible. It was like inflating.

"What?" her mother asked.

That was the secret: it was the wish to be looked at that had undone her concentration. Next time she was sure she would know what to do differently.

"You had a question?"

"Yes." Giordana paused.

"Why am I not surprised? You always have a question."

"What's an old soul?"

Her mother had been a nurse for twelve years, and that meant not much caught her off-guard. She didn't look the least bit disturbed to hear her words come back at her. She talked so much that she didn't always know whom she said what to, anyway.

"You don't let the crappy bits of life sandbag you."

"The bottom drawer details?"

Her mother looked at her as if for the first time that day. "Bottom drawer, top drawer. All drawers. My hope is that when I grow up I'm as cool and beautiful as you are right now." Her mother had once defined cool as Aunt Natalie who, she said, could make perfect sandwiches in the middle of a battlefield. This was what was expected. No one had ever bothered to define beautiful.

"Thank you," Giordana said, though she wasn't sure what for.

"All right, at least you can choose which side of the bed you want."

The alarm went off. Her mother was already in the bathroom.

Giordana reached across the sad excuse for a mattress and over the edge of the metal bed frame to press buttons on the clock till it shut up.

A minute later, her mother was closing the front door, off to look for a job. They really were here to stay.

Another minute later and Alek and Sasha were bouncing on the bed, demanding attention. It was nearly eight o'clock. She burrowed her face into the ancient foam pillow. Alek fluffed her sheet up in the air, making a tent around him and her. He squatted close, bringing his face in front of hers. "I see you!"

She looked at him, his gap-toothed smile and his eyes off centre like a Picasso. A Picasso drawing of a lemur. He had given her the choice – flying or invisibility. Giordana had a vision of them decades in the future – their parents' age – still knowing each other, still connected in a vital way. What if she'd said she wanted to fly?

In a voice that could only be heard under the sheets, she asked him, "Did you know?"

"About what?" He looked confused, genuine. He wanted to play.

"Nothing," Giordana said.

This was entirely hers. She was sure she could have disappeared in front of them, but she didn't want anyone to freak out and tell.

"Boys, come," Peter called from the hall.

Alek asked her, "You'll be here when we get home from camp?"

"Yes."

"Good."

She scattered them by shaking the sheet and they ran for the door.

It would be her and Ben in the house. Natalie had already left for school. She taught primary. *A nurse or a teacher*, her mother had always said. *Those were the choices. These days you have a hundred different careers to explore.* What would Giordana be when she grew up? Invisible.

Mimicking her mother's efficiency, she flattened the sheets and folded the bed into itself. She further minimised their neat stacks, and got dressed. Denim shorts and a red T-shirt made her look, she was sure, like a matching but distant version of Thea, Dee and Emily who were probably, at that exact minute, on their way to the swimming pool. They would lie on towels on the concrete steps till lunchtime. If one of them got super ambitious, they could sit in the shallow end, kicking their legs like old ladies. Then they would split off for their jobs. They would go through the first day assuming Giordana was sick. There could be a call that night – Thea had her own phone in her room – to see if she was okay. Dad, drunk beyond comprehension, would tell whoever called his side of the story. Giordana should have asked Aunt Natalie if she could make the long distance call to Thea today to tell her exactly what was up. Tomorrow. There would be time.

Giordana noticed an ink stain on the pocket of her shorts. Staring at it, she concentrated her thoughts to zap it away. No luck. She didn't want to change her clothes. Putting on something different for a girl like Janelle would represent an extreme failure, a defeat for average girls everywhere. Besides, pretence with new people was profoundly false. The fact was that they had run away from home and she had a spot on her shorts. Trying to make it seem otherwise was a lie. She stared at the stain again without any effect and then put on a different pair of shorts for Janelle.

From the verandah, she could see that the street was still. A few cars sat in driveways and not even a breeze through the evenly spaced trees. Giordana went back inside to make a quick round of the house without the house knowing. She lessened herself. Looked down: no legs, no arms. Ace. She trusted her senses to know she was not just a floating head. Proprioception, the feeling of your body in space. What was it called when your body was there but not there? She took the stairs with her hands up, as if it was all a balancing act.

Peter and Natalie's bedroom door was closed. A scan through their bathroom cabinets and dresser drawers might have been illuminating, but turning the knob was more of a breach than she could justify. Mental note: learn how to pass through doors. The boys' room, available though it was, would have held no secrets. The study door was ajar. Ben's clothes had exploded everywhere and his belongings weren't much of a mystery either. Before leaving, her mother had told Giordana to make sure he tidied up today. If he was able to score his own room, he shouldn't need to be told to make his bed. Giordana kicked his backpack across the floor, further scattering his mess. Like he would notice.

Ben was in the kitchen, eating cereal and humming like an idiot. Because he was older, he had probably been told about the plan to leave. He was injustice itself.

Right in the middle of the kitchen, she became visible.

He glanced up in her direction. "Hey."

He had missed her entrance. That was it. She would never show him again. He wasn't worth it.

"So, what are you going to do today?" she asked.

"Let's check my schedule." He stared into space. "After this, I'll see what our evil corporate rulers have put on television. Then around lunchtime I'll make a sandwich. Big day."

"We need to get to know the neighbourhood. Figure out what's close by. We'll have to get jobs too, if we're going to be here awhile."

"Yeah. I'm concerned," Ben said, pretending to read Uncle Peter's newspaper.

"You think we'll be here for a while?"

"Don't know, Mary-Joe. We're here now."

She was done. "I'm going out with Janelle."

"Isn't that a bit fast for you? Have you even had your first date yet?" He went back to humming.

He was so easy to ignore. "I'm going to learn the neighbourhood. There must be stuff to get into around here."

"Good luck."

He continued to gaze at the paper. Such an arsehole.

"Clean up when you're done," Giordana said, closing the container of milk and putting it back in the fridge.

The doorbell rang. She turned and left without waiting for him to roll his eyes.

Giordana was lucky it was the girl with the hyper-conscious looks who was taking her around. After all, it could have been the local geek providing the tour and that would weigh down whatever hope of a future Giordana might have here.

Fate was decided by other people and by accidents like this. Giordana was living with her aunt and uncle because a long time ago her mother had fallen in love with her father. Why? What random event made *that* happen?

Janelle showed off her house as they passed by. It was smaller than Aunt Natalie's. She led Giordana on a dozen shortcuts between yards that they could bike across without getting yelled at or barked at. None of the kids they passed did more than glance in their direction when they biked through. Still, Janelle knew what was going on inside every bedroom. Who was getting divorced, who was strapped to an oxygen tank, who had crashed their car into a tree on purpose.

"That's sad," Giordana said, as she was presented with each new tragedy.

"Why?" Janelle finally asked. "Did it happen to you?"

They walked the bikes through a park. There was a lung-shaped lake at the centre of it with trails on either side that meandered up to open lawns with picnic tables. Ducks, for Christ's sake, she thought, channelling her father. There was a quiet nook between some trees where, Janelle told her, older kids went to drink and smoke and screw.

Some were there, playing frisbee on one of the lawns. A boy and girl – the serious romantics of their crowd, no doubt – were lying nearby on a big red blanket. The boy was tickling the girl's chin with pieces of grass. It looked like they were trying to see how long she could go without cracking up.

Giordana asked, "Are they the best-looking ones of their friends and that's why they're together or am I imagining that because they're in love?"

"Don't be weird," Janelle said, which Giordana took as *Don't be pitiful.* It was practically a demand to change the subject, but it made Giordana want to go deeper.

"Sorry, I've never had a boyfriend and it looks – impossible," she said, further underlining her inequality with Janelle. She was surprised how little she cared about the impression she was making. If Janelle didn't like it, Giordana could always vanish. She could watch this couple tease each other for hours.

"Have you had one?" Giordana finally asked.

"For three months. Last year. We didn't flaunt it like those two, I can promise you that."

So Janelle didn't see herself like those two either. It was pleasing to think she and Janelle would handle love the same way.

"How old was he?"

"My age. He still is. He went for a younger woman, fifteen."

"I'm fifteen," Giordana said fearlessly, noting that at least theoretically nothing was stopping her from achieving a boyfriend. "Is it awful when you see them together?"

"It's not that big a school. They're hard to avoid."

"No one since then?"

"Nope."

She tried to picture Janelle leaning up to nuzzle Uncle Peter, his hands going for her breasts. Suddenly he was the evil one and she was the innocent. "No one?"

"Don't be weird."

That was proof enough that there was nothing going on. For all of her mother's praise, Giordana did have good intuition about people.

By lunchtime, she had told Janelle about Dad's drinking, the fights with neighbours that came with it, and how it had forced them to move apartments twice in the last year. She told her about the two different accounts of him leaving his job, about them packing up yesterday afternoon and going without a goodbye. She also told her what she didn't think she could ever tell Thea or Emily or Dee: that they were broke. As a family they had been struggling, but now they were like the desperate cousins in Jane Austen, without the yearly allowance. Whatever her mother could make was all they would have. She would definitely have to go back to six shifts a week.

"Sounds like leaving was the right way for her to go," Janelle said. It felt like a slap, her new friend taking her mother's side. And on something so big, something that Giordana herself wasn't even sure of. This was probably why her mother never told her the plan in the first place.

They biked beyond the neighbourhood and Janelle showed her a row of shops, followed by a big supermarket with an even bigger car park and a McDonald's. There were 'help wanted' signs in the windows of both. How would a job there compare to scooping ice-cream in the middle of a city?

When Janelle was ahead of her by one full street, Giordana tried a little test. She and the bike disappeared. As if to tell her how foolish this was, a driver came around a curve behind her and she realised it would be safer, as her father used to command, to stay where she could be seen. In plain view again, she wondered if there was a way this could make her rich. That would solve everything.

They wound their way back to Aunt Natalie's street. Giordana felt sorry for Janelle, stuck here with only the neighbour's niece as a friend.

"Thanks for the guided tour. You didn't have to."

"Peter and Natalie have always been good to me. We could do another ride tomorrow."

"Where will we go?"

"Same places, I guess."

Ruth wasn't home yet and Ben was out, so Giordana spent the afternoon sitting on the verandah reading. Even though it wasn't that cold, she wrapped herself in a crocheted quilt because it made her feel like an old dowager. An old dowager reading *The Love Machine,* which she'd found in the hall. This super-charming guy, hunky and brainy, was ploughing his way through a lot of women who were disposable, at least to him. Giordana didn't understand what they wanted from a man who was such a slut. It didn't sound like a good plan to her. A lot of the novels with covers like this one featured guys who behaved like pigs till they found feelings for the right woman. But what about all those other women that got dumped along the way? Who did they end up with? Dad.

Giordana saw her friendship with Janelle blossoming into an apprenticeship. Janelle's willingness to instruct, Giordana's eagerness to learn. She wanted to be Janelle's special case, a kind of virgin outreach program. Giordana's power would make them equal and keep Janelle interested. If Janelle organised it, Giordana would even consider robbing a bank.

Natalie brought the boys home from camp and Giordana volunteered to watch them for a few hours. The truth was the boys didn't need her much, but Giordana wanted to sound helpful. Sasha stayed upstairs, but Alek was eager to take her around the neighbourhood.

"Once we leave the house, we're free, but there are a variety of dangers everywhere."

It was like going through the streets with Janelle, but on a different plane of existence. When he wasn't singing some made-up marching song, he kept a steady dialogue going, spinning out a story that turned all the houses into the faces of giants and turned the ground they were walking on into their barely buried bodies. Giordana led him through the first few shortcuts that Janelle had showed her. Alek wasn't the least bit impressed and took off through a maze of new ones. Keeping up with him was expected. She didn't remember being like this when she was little. The only one in her house who was allowed to live in their own world was Dad. He always got to be the kid.

"To get around all of them we must be snakes!"

With urgency and slinky arms, Alek led her along the perimeter of a dozen backyards. What if she showed off her power to him? If she held him, could she make him disappear too? They could get past the giants together. No, it was fun enough to watch him make it all up. They stomped on giant fingers, they kicked at giant eyeballs, they pinched giant noses.

Eventually, Alek circled them back home and charged through the front door.

Still breathless in the hall, he said, "Thanks for playing with me, but I need a little down time now." He ditched her at the foot of the stairs, thumping up to his room.

Natalie and Peter were getting dinner ready. The smell of butter and garlic and onions filled the house. Easy stuff – Thea's mother did it all the time – but Giordana's mother usually microwaved. Tonight though, Ruth was racing around the kitchen, making a huge deal about setting the table with napkin swans and cut flowers from the backyard. Giordana wondered if she should be overdoing it too.

Ben hadn't returned from the pool, but their mother insisted they start. Over dinner, she tried to tell everyone about her promising discussions with the human resources people at the nearby hospital. Alek interrupted and ultimately ran the show with his crazy questions.

"What if metal grew hair and Dad not only had to shave his face, but also shave the refrigerator every day?" Uncle Peter found an answer for each one – some of them followed Alek's logic, some of them explained the real world. Giordana's father had once slapped down one of her questions with "curiosity killed the cat". She was furious at him then and again now for silencing her – and with such a lame line. Peter was attentive. She was sorry she had thought he would bang the babysitter.

Afterwards, it seemed to be assumed that Giordana would clean up. She went at it the way a scullery maid would, cleaning far beyond the meal's mess. It was almost dark when Ben finally came back. He ate leftovers while she finished scrubbing hand prints that probably belonged to Alek and Sasha from the refrigerator door.

Ben told her he had seen Janelle at the pool and they'd hung out. "You didn't tell her about Dad, did you?" he asked. Talking to outsiders about family business would be a completely wrong thing to do.

"A little. Not much. Why?"

"I told her we were here for the summer, for vacation," Ben said.

"What did she say to that?"

"She said she wished she could go to the city for a visit sometime."

"What did you say?"

"I told her we should try and make it happen."

Giordana didn't understand anybody. "And she'll stay with us at our penthouse overlooking the waterfront?"

"Shut up. I'm meeting up with her again tonight."

Before she could even ask, Ben told her, "You can't tag along." He had the asinine grin of someone who thought he was the Love Machine but wasn't.

Giordana was wounded, but content with the knowledge that he was not at all in Janelle's league. He didn't exercise and Janelle already knew he was bogus. When Ben left the room, Giordana cleaned up after him too, wiping his chair as if she were wiping his conversation from her mind.

As she hung the tea towel over the edge of the sink, she heard a familiar sound. She went invisible, and slyly swung open the door into the living room. It was what she thought: her mother, doubled over crying on the sofa, next to Natalie. The sobbing was muffled by her hands, as if she wanted to be heard but also wanted to keep down the noise. "The things he said to me were so mean, so needlessly mean." Her words struggled out.

"I never planned on failing like this," she said.

"You couldn't have known," Natalie said.

"Don't say that. I could have. You would have known. I didn't listen. It was all there, but I never took the time to listen."

Natalie pulled Ruth close, shielding her from harm. They stayed like this for a long time. Giordana hadn't longed for a sister in a while, but she wanted one then. She tried to imagine other scenes in her mother and Natalie's history when this position would have helped them. She knew Uncle Peter had broken up with Natalie once, right before he proposed. Her mother had consoled her then and persuaded her to write to him. They lived happily ever after.

Natalie didn't say a word while Ruth rolled back and forth in her embrace. This was another silent method of Natalie's that was worth remembering. It didn't deny her mother's failure but it didn't make fake promises of a gleaming future either. Giordana's heart had been a little bit broken last year. She had asked Derek from English to a movie and he said no, smirking at the invitation. Her mother's idea of comfort was to fill her ears with declarations of her rare charms, all the wonderful dates she would have and other crap, but a year passed and exactly nothing had happened to her. Giordana vowed that if her mother came crying to her, she would stay absolutely quiet and put her arms around her the same way that Natalie was holding her now.

Giordana walked around the far side of the staircase, making herself visible so that she could enter the room. Her mother looked up from her sister's embrace and held out an arm to Giordana. "Over here, darling."

"Am I interrupting?" Giordana asked.

"No. I'm just sad about Dad."

Giordana approached, eager to hear whatever her mother had to reveal. What was going to happen next? Was she going to call him? He must have known where they were. She wanted facts and feelings. Instead Ruth closed the topic off with a smile. She wrapped her hands around each of Giordana's wrists and said, "At least I have you, my gorgeous girl."

Her mother settled down eventually; she and Natalie were drinking some kind of healthy tea and talking about their childhood. Peter was upstairs getting the boys into bed.

Ben left for Janelle's. A minute later, Giordana announced, "I'm going out for a walk." Her mother gave a regal back-in-control nod, as if the sole reason for ending her marriage was to bring Giordana somewhere placid enough that she could take long walks in the evening.

As soon as she was out of the house, she turned invisible and bolted after her brother, sprinting across lawns to get in front of him. Ben made it to Janelle's front steps, straightened his posture and rang the doorbell. Giordana was next to him. Like it was some nightclub, Janelle opened the door, looked around, and pulled him in. Giordana considered squeezing in but she didn't think quickly enough. Janelle shut the door.

Giordana paced on the pavement, waiting for them to come out. Every other front yard had jasmine growing somewhere, as regular as air fresheners. The reason it was safe on these streets was because there was no one there. They were all inside watching television. The hum of air conditioning fought with the pulse of cicadas. The former, she realised, cocooned everyone from the latter.

After five minutes, she looked into the front room and it was empty. Had they gone out a back door? She snuck around to the other side of the house, to the only lighted room she could see.

They were there, on a chaise longue. Janelle's top was off and Ben's hands were all over her bra.

As Thea said: *You can't spell chastity without tit.*

Giordana was mesmerised. There was no discussion, no negotiation, and no polite protests. They were open-mouth kissing with equal force. Together, they unhooked Janelle's bra. They didn't even know each other, but – Giordana knew from many paperbacks – you didn't need to.

Ben was grinding his pelvis against Janelle's. Exactly as Emily had reported. It was very animal. Janelle didn't look like she cared. In fact, she was the first to open her shorts, pulling his hand there, directing the action fully south of her belly button. Giordana couldn't see it and had no urge to pass through walls for better access, but it was all happening. There was no slowing down to talk feelings. She was embarrassed for Janelle. Giordana would never go this far with a boy who told her he was here on vacation. Was Janelle doing this because Peter and Natalie had been good to her? It didn't look like that was on her mind.

Ben stood up and at first Giordana thought some kind of decency had seized his conscience, but what he was doing was pulling down his pants. Watching her brother was the opposite of okay, but she decided that her invisibility provided some sort of technicality that allowed it. Besides, it was educational. Anthropological.

Ben's erection sprang up. Ick. It looked like the ones in Thea's father's dirty magazines, but more naked because it was real life. Or because it was her brother's. Janelle grabbed for it on an instinct that Giordana couldn't fathom. There were a few words exchanged and Ben leaned over to reach into the back pocket of his pants. Absurd. His soft body driven by this rigid dick pointing to the ceiling. He retrieved a foil-packet and stood again proud, almost posing with it for Janelle who nodded like she was happy about something. In the next movement, he had unwrapped the condom and was pulling it on. Then he pulled her on. Her face showed a flare of adjustment, but then she was right at home.

Janelle's expression became blank and rushed. What did she think of him? What did he think of her? Was anyone thinking about the two per cent failure rate of condoms? It was all a problem Giordana had hoped would be solved by watching. It wasn't. And she didn't think she really wanted to hear.

Ben shined with sweat. Janelle pushed him off and he did it some more from a different angle. Without saying anything to her, he shuffled their position, as if he didn't want to miss this chance to try the whole zodiac. Suddenly he held Janelle still for a long moment. His eyes closed and his body shook, as if he was struggling with balance. Giordana knew what this was. Unbelievable. She stared at their faces – her brother's eyes closed, Janelle looking self-consciously around the room – but they didn't tell her anything about what had just happened. Her brother went limp. Janelle looked neither here nor there about the whole thing. The Love Machine wouldn't have stopped until Janelle was helpless and quivering. Her body looked more ordinary now. Her hair was flat. It was all over, so she climbed over him to leave, maybe to get a glass of water. The whole thing looked more like a workout than anything else.

With Janelle out of the room, Giordana was left watching Ben's naked, self-satisfied grossness. He mopped up with a tissue. She felt more alone with him like this and she backed away from the window until Janelle returned. The two of them squeezed next to each other on the chaise longue again, sort of dressed, sort of paying attention to each other, and sort of staring into space. Though Giordana couldn't hear what they were saying, they apparently had things to talk about. An enigma.

Giordana went home and showered. She crept onto her side of the sofa bed, careful not to jostle her mother who had already turned off the light.

The deafening silence of the suburbs made it hard for Giordana to relax. There was so much to process. She fidgeted under the covers. It was as if the stillness around her made her questions more important. What had Ben and Janelle said at the swimming pool that made that scene possible? Was he actually appealing or was he simply her only choice? What if Giordana couldn't see her brother clearly and if he was actually hot? If Ben and Janelle were going to be a couple, would Giordana be able to be friends with Janelle? She couldn't see how. Most of all, she didn't understand what made Janelle go from being so "don't be weird" to being on her back and panting in the space of an afternoon? *That* was what was weird. No logic. All of them said and did whatever they wanted, whenever they wanted. Under the sheet, her mother turned and reached over, gliding her fingers through her daughter's hair. Half asleep, she told Giordana, "Everything's fine."

Riding the bus invisible wasn't stealing. The three-hour trip to the city would happen whether or not she was on it and Giordana didn't weigh all that much. She didn't even hog a seat because as soon as anyone walked over to where she was, she sprang right up so that they wouldn't sit on her lap. Best of all, she could stare. It was awesome. She watched women, wondering about their bodies. She watched men, wondering what they had done last night. She studied the faces of the most handsome men and paired herself with them on a hotel bed somewhere, gazing at each other as they rocked together towards – as she'd read one particular orgasm described – oblivion. It sounded nice.

Arriving at the main station, she stayed invisible but had to keep alert to not cause trouble. The streets were filled with more crowds and hazards than she remembered. It was a big game of hopscotch getting to Thea's house. Occasionally she would bump into someone and they would shoot a dirty look to the closest person they could see. If she'd wanted to, she could have incited a riot. She dodged people in work clothes, mothers with strollers, homeless people with their bags of stuff, and dog owners with a few spooked dogs that seemed to look directly at her.

Giordana looked in Thea's front windows and rang the bell. If Thea had opened the door without asking who was there – which she sometimes did despite knowing better – Giordana would sneak in. But no one came to the door.

She walked the three blocks to Sprinkles and that's

where she found her posse. Three girls wearing party dresses and eye shadow in the middle of the day. Like an ad for adolescence. They had probably come there to look for Giordana and been told that she hadn't shown up for work. They had evidently lived through the trauma and were having ice-creams. Thea had clearly bought double scoops for all of them with money her parents had intended to be used for food that week. Emily was wearing Giordana's yellow dress. What Emily liked to call *the mysteries of sleepovers* always managed to work in her favour.

Three girls, not very different from Giordana, but completely clueless, acting like they were on a break from making a music video. They were being so loud. They had their high heels up on each other's laps. They probably had cocktails for breakfast. The urge to sit down with them, to continue as if the summer hadn't been fatally interrupted, was wiped out by the desire to not be seen by the boss she had left without warning. Plus, there was the promise of listening in on her friends.

There were no surprises. They were talking about people walking by, about the mascara Emily had shoplifted last week, about all the dirty dishes they had left in the kitchen. About nothing.

If she were in a party dress and high heels, Giordana was sure she wouldn't have been this frivolous. If she had slept over the night before, she might have had a sip of one of the blender concoctions (even though she had looked at her father on more than one night and vowed never to drink). But she would not have been so giggly.

A need to say goodbye to them was one of the reasons she snuck onto the bus that morning, but that had evaporated. It was replaced by the thought that her friends should be paying closer attention to real things, those random events that could change the arithmetic of their lives. The girls weren't talking about Dee almost getting pregnant by Connor last month. They weren't talking about Emily, who was going to get caught stealing some day soon. They weren't talking about Thea who was cushioned from the world by money – a fate that was starting to look pretty good. And worst of all, there was no mention of their missing friend. They probably just thought she was sick. Or they didn't care that she wasn't around.

Giordana grabbed the side of their table and lifted it, enough to tip their water. As the glasses slid close to the edge, she let go, slamming it back down. The water poured off the table and they scrambled to clean it up before anyone saw. The girls were freaked, but looking at each other kept them smiling. Giordana waited half a minute and did it again, harder. That made them silent. *There*, Giordana thought: *that's what the world is like.*

On her father's street, the creepy guy was sitting on a car.

One day last year, when she was walking home with groceries, he came up to her and said, "Whoa. You're nearly ripe, aren't you?" Close enough now to smell his ripeness – cigarette skin and a sunny day of drinking beer – she took his can from the top of the car, disappearing it and then making it reappear in the rubbish on the street corner. She watched him hunt all over the street, cursing creation for having stolen his drink.

Using her keys to get into their building, she climbed the three flights to their apartment. It was the middle of the afternoon so there was a fifty-fifty chance her father was awake. As if she were cracking a safe, she listened at the metal door for any sounds before turning the key to let herself in without a click.

There was the possibility that he would be sitting in his wicker armchair by the television, deadened, and watching the door to the apartment open and close on its own. If he did, she hoped he would chalk the vision up to too much whisky.

All the blinds had been raised, as if to highlight the need for a good cleaning of all the surfaces.

His chair was empty. Maybe he was invisible too.

What had she come here for? Every single thing looked second-hand, like it had been left behind on purpose. An enormous fruit bowl her parents had been given for their wedding, the painting of the knots of a rose bush that Natalie had done when she and Ruth were girls, even a box of chocolates on the kitchen counter that were being saved for some happy occasion that wasn't going to come. The place smelled like an op-shop.

There were two half-full bottles of Jim Beam, one in the bedroom and one in the hall. Giordana carried them both to the kitchen and threw them into the sink, breaking them, splashing everywhere. The room seized with the essence of Dad.

He would come back from wherever he was and stare at the shards in the sink. Maybe he would think he had done it himself in some theatrical bid to quit. Maybe he would take it as a sign and never drink again. Maybe he would sell the punchbowl for as much as he could get so that he could keep drinking for another few days. Maybe he would cut his wrists with the broken glass at the mind-boggling idiocy of losing his family over booze, or over losing the booze. Giordana pretended she didn't care which path he took, that she'd be detached enough to make perfect triangle sandwiches with the crusts cut off. To prove her toughness, she grabbed a handful of the chocolates and pushed them into her mouth, strawberry cream, coconut and coffee truffle all munched together.

Still chewing, only tasting the sugar, she went to her bedroom. Her red backpack was hooked on the back of the door. It was the house-on-fire decision: what do you take with you when you have less than a minute? How much can you carry? Sifting through the room with a glance, she felt restrained as she only picked up her photo album. Even its pinkness was juvenile now, but she wanted the pictures as proof. Heading through the living room again, she wolfed down another handful of chocolates.

Her father's half-hearted footsteps echoed on the stairs.

Without even thinking about it, she backed into the hallway near her bedroom and went invisible. It would take concentration to stay that way with him in the room. His keys clanged on the side of the door.

He came in, alone and aimless at two in the afternoon. A little disoriented, a little disinterested in it all. When Thea met him for the first time, she had said with innocent surprise, "My dad's forty too, but he's not as leathery in the face."

He had a newspaper and a bag of groceries with him, if you called a six-pack groceries. It all looked like an ordinary afternoon, except for the placid expression, which she had never seen before. She recognised it immediately as the feeling of sanctuary you have when you come home to an empty apartment.

He would never call them again.

What had she expected? It had always been her mother's job to mend but she wasn't going to do it anymore. So this was it, right here. When would Giordana see him next? Would he show up at her graduation, at her wedding? Would she meet him on his deathbed or maybe go to his funeral? Maybe he would try to kidnap her, like divorced dads did on the news. No. He had the anger but he wasn't, her mother was fond of saying, particularly goal-oriented.

Giordana let him see her. "Dad?"

Barely surprised to find her there, his eyes went to the photo album in her hand. He nodded. "The minute you left, you remembered what you forgot, am I right?"

Sometimes his rhetorical questions were tricks. Giordana took a second to think.

"Am I right?" He was in her face.

"You're right."

"I'm right."

She stayed in the hallway by the kitchen, not knowing where to stand. Her father started to clear the older newspapers and cans from around his chair, as if that had been his plan for the afternoon. Not looking up, he told her, "You'll be a grown-up soon and you'll have your own relationships. You'll see that we did this for you too. Staying together would have been no favour to you and Ben. And no picnic for us."

On other afternoons when he spouted off like this, she had been respectful, acting as if she was being enlightened to the facts of adulthood. *Noblesse oblige,* she had thought when she used to nod, keeping her opinions to herself; but now she wondered who the good manners protected.

He nodded intently, checking that she was with him on this. She kept her expression flat, unsympathetic. That was reason enough for him to stop what he was doing. He took the beer he had bought and came towards the kitchen to put it in the fridge. It was what he wanted to do anyway.

"We're not being selfish. We're being realistic," he said as he passed her, not caring if she believed him or not. "You'll see."

"Tell yourself whatever you want," Giordana said.

He stopped. He didn't face her but he lingered, challenging her to say more. She looked at his stubble, the flecks of white. He must have stopped shaving the day they left. And showering, too.

Her head turned back and forth in a slow *no* – the same way her mother did when she'd had enough. It denied whatever it was he was saying. It denied the person he had become.

He recognised the gesture and waved his arm at the door. "Get out then, if you don't approve. Ask your mother exactly who left who."

Getting ready to say goodbye forever, she took two shaky steps away from him.

"You know what happens if you leave like this?" Without using force, just his advancing steps, he cornered her against the door. "None of you better come back. Tell her it's too late for any patch job. The air's already come out of the tyre, the tyre's torn. It's totally flat. Tell her that," he said.

"I'll tell her."

"And tell your brother too. He's going to have to learn and he won't learn anything from her. Tell him this: a marriage is two different individuals trying to be the same one. Humans weren't made that way."

"I want to go," she said.

"Tell me you understand what I said."

"No. Let me out of here," she said, her hand on the doorknob. He barely budged.

She tried to push him off and he pinned her arms. The shoulder of her shirt tore a little. He didn't care and pressed her harder, as if that would make her listen.

Giordana lunged at his chest to make him move, pushing him around till he was the one against the door. He was still blocking her way.

He laughed at her effort, but he was getting impatient. "You don't get it," he said. "That's what the problem is. You're going to grow up believing whatever she tells you. I feel sorry for you, I do."

"I feel sorry for you too," she said, crying, pulling on the doorknob pointlessly.

His eyes were shining too – with sadness, with anger? – but he wasn't letting go. "Would it kill you to stay and listen to your father a minute?"

He wanted to talk more. All these adults expected her to console them for screwing up her life.

He said, "It'll be all right, darling. It will." His arms were around her, acting as if she were the one who wanted a hug. She didn't.

She pulled one arm free, raised the photo album up

and brought its hard edge down against his forehead. He stopped to feel the spot she'd hit.

"Hey!" he said, his hands up in a truce.

She roared into him, slamming her body against his chest again and again, trying to get him away from the door, even as he was trying to calm her. Finally she pushed herself against him with such force that at the point of contact everything went still and suffocating.

It was dark for a flash, but then there was air again.

She was standing in the hall, breathing hard. She had gone through him, gone through the door.

If you want something badly enough, it turns out.

Behind her she heard him call her name into the apartment. Mystified, he called her again, and swore. He opened the door behind her as she vanished, and he yelled right into her ear, "Where are you?"

The ride back was easier. Giordana caught an express, which had fewer people trying to sit on her. She had two seats to herself for most of the way and sat there, her hands crossed over the photo album to keep it invisible. It had lost some of its value in the fight with her father. It had gone from being a girly keepsake to a weapon. Were all the pictures inside similarly tainted? Would they still show birthday parties and school trips or would they show a screwed up family and a girl who was desperate to escape? She resolved not to look at the photos for a while.

Reading the highway signs was the only way to tell where she was. Buildings and tunnels gave way to trees and then shadowy buildings and then neon. The small towns dragged on, dark silhouettes on a dark sky.

Even so, if she stared hard she could see that the bus was keeping still and everything else was racing past her. Giordana's friends and their sleepovers, her mother out begging for work at the hospital, Ben and Janelle on a blanket in the bushes, her father out buying more alcohol or joining AA. They were all separate, scattering like planets without even asking each other if it was okay.

It was nearly ten when she made it back to the house. Spying first could have helped her gauge what sort of scene she was in for, but she didn't see the point. Ben had come back from the pool almost as late. Any lecture she was going to get was irrelevant. She didn't have to listen to anyone.

Her mother and Natalie were sitting on the verandah. They leapt off the sofa like they were synchronised, and rushed up to meet her.

Giordana walked up the steps saying, "I should have called, but I didn't have any change."

"That's not the point," they said in near unison.

"Where were you?" her mother demanded.

Giordana saw Ben and Janelle sitting on the sofa watching TV, close to each other, almost touching. Ben grinned at Giordana because she was in trouble. She kept her grin about him to herself. She called to Janelle, "I'm sorry I stood you up this morning. I had to go home for this." She waved the little photo album.

"It's okay," Janelle said, half-watching the television, probably adding this new neighbourhood gossip to her repertoire.

Her mother went off. "Home? Giordana! Your father could have done anything, do you understand? He could have kept you there and all of this could have become ten times worse."

"You've brought us here now, so it already is ten times worse."

"Don't tell me what's right. You shouldn't have run away like that."

"I didn't run away. And what was Dad going to do, anyway?"

Uncle Peter stood at the back of the hallway, waiting for his turn to play the father. "Your mother, all of us, we were extremely worried. We didn't know where you went or what had happened to you."

"Nothing happened to me."

Her mother said, "I've been waiting for hours for the phone to ring." She sniffed the air. "Is that alcohol?"

"I broke all his bottles in the sink. Some must have got on me."

"Oh baby," her mother said, hugging her. Giordana knew exactly where this was headed. The upset was going to turn into an opera, which meant Giordana would spend the evening assuring her mother that leaving him was a brilliant thing to do and that it didn't hurt a bit.

"And what's this?" Natalie asked, holding the rip in her shirt.

"I don't know."

Peter piped up and came forward, "'I don't know' isn't an acceptable answer in this house." He looked in at Ben and said, "You too. Come here," waving him into the hall. "I know you've both been living through difficult times at home and being here is not what you envisioned for your-selves but you're both nearly adults."

Alek appeared at the top of the stairs wearing only his Superman underpants. Giordana had to think serious thoughts to keep from cracking up at the sight of him. His little legs were doing a jig, as if there was music playing somewhere.

These people around her loved her and that's why they were so worried. Uncle Peter was trying to be sensible. He was looking out for her. She had to remember that.

He went on, "While you are here, we will not tolerate bad behaviour. And we've got a wide definition for that. It includes drinking alcohol, taking drugs, not doing chores when asked, and going off without leaving a note."

With one hand on his hip, Alek wagged a finger at Giordana in a tsk-tsk rhythm. She had to limit herself to only quick glances at him or Peter would have turned around and seen. Alek's attitude would have made him go up another octave.

The boy's face was sedating. It said, *This is temporary.* All of it – Uncle Peter, the house, the street, the country, the world. Any single element might change in an instant. Because it was pushed one day, because it wanted to or because it was simply time to go. The good news was that she could do the same. And that would cause other changes to happen, things she couldn't imagine. Someday she and Alek would be grown-ups and remember this together. They would be somewhere else entirely. France, the moon.

Her mother took over, "You have to keep in mind that we are guests here and there will be no more disrespect and no more vanishing acts. Is that clear?"

Everything was clear. In another minute it might not be. That was clear too.

Her mother put her hands on Giordana's shoulders. "Is any of this sinking in?"

Natalie

At the end of what should have been a peaceful Sunday lunch, she and Peter had tried to discuss with Alek a stream of absences from school and from the swimming team, but after five minutes of sulky silence, they were nowhere. Peter, caught in some father-son game, would be willing to let the battle go on indefinitely. Alek was content to win through silence, which of course twisted Peter into bigger knots. The entire confrontation drained Natalie and she wished it would end. Her sole desire for the afternoon: a nap on the verandah, a half-opened book in her hand.

Alek stretched his arms open across the table towards his parents. It was the position of truce but not the spirit: "If I say anything, I'm in trouble. If I don't say anything, I'm in trouble. I'm not saying anything." And then he checked out, as per usual.

When Peter replied that he wasn't to leave the room until his conduct was explained in full, a jolt of common sense took over. She pushed her chair back, excused herself and went straight upstairs to Alek's bedroom. In the back of his wardrobe, behind the curtain of old coats, she found his porn burrow and, from underneath it, retrieved the navy leather-bound diary. She was appalled at what she might be unleashing.

For months she had known of its existence – once even flipping through its pages – but she had prided herself on having the appropriate detachment to let him become his own man. Her present weakness shamed her. Evidently not enough. She had already committed the crime – taken it from his room and locked herself with it in the hall bathroom – so remorse would achieve little. An old shoelace tailed out of the book as a placeholder. She rationalised: there was a defensible and very straight line from the act of breastfeeding to this. She turned the shower on for the noise, braced herself for unimaginable adolescent horrors, and opened to the saved page.

It was blank.

There were eleven blank ones before that. They had been bent open and creased down, as if he had spent as much time composing on these as the previous ones that were filled with his scrawl. She flipped through again, expecting a message to fall out or materialise from the emptiness. She held the pages up to the light to see if they had been etched in some way to hide his words from his brother or his prying mother. They weren't. Perhaps he'd used lemon juice, Natalie and Ruth's trick for writing notes to each other for one entire year when they were young. (Long before Sasha or Alek had a hint of chin hair, Natalie taught the boys the lemon juice trick – invisible at the time of writing, revealed with heat. But she knew, even as she held a page over the toaster to make the words materialise for them, that they would never find any use for the trick; they were, alas, boys, and didn't have as many secrets to share.) Holding the journal close to her face, she could see the pages were smooth and had never been dampened.

Visible written entries stopped twelve days earlier. The last of these were about Alek's best friend Ned, who had recently had sex with his girlfriend – for the second time, apparently. Ned must have shared the specifics of anatomy and procedure with Alek because they had all been recorded. The embarrassment of detail convinced Natalie that Alek was still a virgin. Although he was only sixteen, it felt like another milestone he was skipping. Months ago she had decided, or at any rate accepted, that he and Vicenta, who had been 'hanging out' since the school year began, were ready. Natalie had more than once caught them furtively holding hands while they watched TV. She didn't know the parents well, but she trusted Vicenta. She was a year ahead of Alek, which Natalie took to be a fact in support of his maturity. She was pretty, but not too. And Spanish, which Natalie admitted to having a suspect appreciation for, if only for its own novelty in their neighbourhood. Plus, Natalie was confident that, after much school board debate, the sex education teacher was being fiercely explicit about the perils of pregnancy and, now, HIV. Both kids would have been smart enough to use condoms.

But at first glance, no mention of Vicenta in the diary. Evidence of any sex life at all could have explained his sudden neglect of other areas. Natalie looked back a few pages, through ruminations on some unforgivable demands of his English teacher and a few lines from a poem or song – 'drop me far, drop me deep / leave me just my soul to keep'. She didn't think they were all that pleasant, but she couldn't imagine that it represented a bridging step to drug addiction. She was eager to find Vicenta somewhere in there.

Three days before the writing stopped: 'Vicenta (love) says I am loco perfect.' Natalie assumed this was a compliment and slammed the pad closed with revulsion for having read this much.

What had she been expecting to find? *I cut school to rob 7-Elevens* in his blocky handwriting? No such clarity. Textbook boy stuff with a few empty pages. She turned off the shower.

Downstairs, Peter sounded like he was finishing up his reprimand. Thankfully, Sasha – one year older than Alek, and infinitely more social – wasn't home for this or he would have found a way to mock Alek or Peter or all of them.

Natalie opened Alek's bedroom door, took the three steps to the wardrobe, reburied the journal, and backed out into the hall in one neat movement, asserting to herself all the while that it was her house and she was the keeper of its contents. Alek came up the stairs as she pretended to be walking out of the bathroom. His eyes were on the carpet. He couldn't have been aware of her trespass.

"How did it go?" she asked him, with a conspiratorial kindness that repulsed her.

He looked up, his eyes red, and gave her a sarcastic brow-raise. "You could have stayed."

"I'm sorry, love." She knew she hadn't exactly played the role of his liberator in the whole scenario.

"Why did you leave me with him?"

For expedience. If she could find out what was keeping Alek from his responsibilities – by any means necessary – surely she could help.

"I'm sorry," she said, "I was having a hot flush." It was cheap, she knew.

"So you had a hot shower?"

"No, I—" and she followed his eyes to the steam coming out of the bathroom.

That fumble was all the proof he needed of her false-ness. The uselessness of adults. He gave her a grim dismissal. "Whatever you two want," he said. "You own me, for the next few years at least."

"Don't be dramatic. We're trying to—"

Alek abandoned her for his room, pulling hard on the door so that air blew against her face, but stopping right at the end so that it closed with barely a sound, circumventing the house rule against slamming.

Natalie let out a sigh that matched it, but inside she was transformed into a fountain of frustration. Like a hot flush, but invigorating. She wanted to force her way in, push him to the ground – tenderly, of course, protecting his head – and sit on his chest and start demanding answers. The surge of violence startled her. Teenagers.

Peter climbed the stairs, looking every bit as worked up as Alek had looked worked over. Hushed, he met her two steps from the top.

She said, "I'm sorry, sweet. I had to escape from the two of you together. You were getting nothing from each other. What happened?"

"What do you imagine? You left, he got upset without you to bat for him. But he held tight. Didn't tell me where he's been going. Not our business, apparently. Doesn't want time off, doesn't want a shrink. Says he'll attend school and swimming without fail from this day onwards. There's no reason to believe what he says and I told him so. From tomorrow, and until we get some idea of what's actually happening inside that head of his, I bring him to school. After work you take him from there to swimming practice and wait for him till he's done. I think that's fair."

"Seems reasonable," she said, although it sounded like thumbscrews. The alibi for her departure from the table was weak and she had no other plan to suggest. Neither of them knew what they were doing for Alek. Increased monitoring was as thoughtful an approach as any.

Natalie spent the afternoon pruning the hell out of the roses. She planted an apple sapling and put in some bulbs for spring. She raked the leaves into a pile that the boys would once have adored, but that was distinctly in the past, so she burned it. While the smoke spun upwards, she weeded. It was as if every thistle was another instance of bad parenting and she tugged with care to be sure she pulled up each of their tiny roots.

An urge to get away led her to drive over to the pond for a walk. The small clearing of sandy beach was empty. It always was, unless it was the absolute swelter of summer. The water was dark and still, except for a few red leaves spinning near the shore. Ordinarily Natalie, too thin and easily chilled, wouldn't have considered it, but she still felt this extra energy inside. She had to burn it off or she would take it out on Alek. What else was the bathing suit in the back of the car for?

She changed behind a tree and walked down to the edge to see how brave she really was. Going under, it was new water. Like when Peter had first brought her to the pond – before the boys, before they had even bought the house. Never a bold swimmer, her habit was to make slow contented circles close to the shore or paddle around with minimal splashing, on lookout for birds or other distractions in the surrounding woods. Not today. Without pausing to adjust to the temperature or marvel at the clarity of the late afternoon light, she swam the length of the pond and back. Ten times, with pure speed. She did ten more laps just as quickly, stopping only because she was starting to worry about the time. She wasn't even out of breath.

"That flame's too high," Peter said.

"Not quite." Natalie rotated the chicken thighs in a sizzling pan. "I had a ridiculously good swim at the pond," she said.

"I should have gone."

"I wonder. I wonder if I would have done as well with anyone else around."

Peter frowned.

She turned off the flame and shook the pan a few times before putting it over a cool burner. "There, done." She reached for his hand. "Suffice it to say that the pleasure for us is in me telling you about it."

"Sufficed."

"It was lovely though. I felt Olympian."

"Wonderful. Hormones?" he suggested.

'No doubt,' Natalie said. "Call the boys."

She may as well have only requested Sasha's attendance. Alek absented himself so thoroughly from the conversation that even Peter gave up on forcing him to engage. Sasha tried, prodding him to gossip about an English teacher they both had who was pregnant, but that went nowhere. Natalie kept watching him through the meal. At times she felt that he was observing her too.

The force that had propelled Natalie across the pond kept her from sleeping. Giving into it at midnight, she wandered the house. A sentinel watching over her men. Peter with his smooth tidal snore, Sasha sleeping sweetly. Alek, with his door closed and light on. Perhaps he was awake with the same bug? No, he had his own concerns. If he could rip through water like Natalie, he would be turning up for swim.

In the morning, Natalie watched Alek get into the car for the enforced ride. He complied, sitting limply in the passenger seat.

At her school, Natalie's ability to work with the chaos of her students was mythic. The afternoon schedule of reading corner followed by art time was a vibration of coordinated productivity. Even the children's ability to colour in appeared to be improving. Later, when the parents came, she provided far more than her usual dose of feedback. The children in their construction paper crowns trudged home, their parents proudly holding hands and carrying all the gold-starred projects. As they scattered, Natalie felt thirsty for more.

She didn't discuss Alek with anyone, even at lunch when one of the other teachers went on and on about her son's chronic lying. Peter wasn't the type to talk about it at work either. The last thing he would mention to the staff of a small local paper would be his own small local news. One time Ruth had called Natalie an uptight suburban lady. Fondly, of course. If she and Peter knew more about Alek, they might be capable of unburdening themselves and commiserating with their peers. Natalie hoped. Had their reserve turned him inwards?

After school, she took a break from corralling first graders into playgroups to call the assistant principal at the high school. Peter had made him complicit with their surveillance. The man duly confirmed Alek's attendance that day.

Natalie drove up the ramp to retrieve him. Alek and Vicenta were sitting on a concrete bench in front of the high school.

He was staring at a patch of trampled grass while Vicenta spoke to him, steadily rocking towards his ear, as if she were insisting on being heard. He maintained his shrugging, evasive expression. Her seriousness seemed to be matched by his vagueness. A disloyal thought bubbled up in Natalie: what was Vicenta even doing with him?

Alek said something that made Vicenta laugh and she punched him on the arm. Her hand lingered on his shoulder. At least they were still together. He wasn't completely adrift. But it didn't explain the blank pages or the absences. He was hiding from all of them.

Cruising slowly closer, Natalie announced herself with a short toot. If the two of them hadn't had sex, it was Alek's choice, she was sure. It was the way Vicenta faced him and the way he turned away. The feeling was confirmed when Vicenta complimented Natalie's extremely ordinary blouse. It was as if she was trying to worm her way into Natalie's good books in order to get closer to Alek. Good luck with that.

Natalie escorted the prisoner to the sports complex at the university, past the outdoor pool to the indoor one where the boys wouldn't get too chilled. Bless their little bodies. It had been a while since Natalie had stood around poolside during practice. The shimmering surface demanded that she dive in, but she was the only parent there. It would have been unseemly. When Ned, nearly Peter's height now and sprouting hair everywhere, gave her a sheepish "Hello," she suppressed the urge to take him aside and interrogate him about Alek.

Across their designated lanes, the clutch of boys displayed the entire bandwidth of male physical development and emotional immaturity. Some were splashing, pushing each other in, yanking on bathers, and swimming crosswise under all the lane dividers. The coach condoned it, telling them to knock it off while chuckling. A few were performing quick, minnow-like laps, springing off the far end and shooting back to the start in one or two breaths. When they completed their circuit, they pushed themselves up, little suburban gods rising from the water, and shivered across the pale blue tiles to see where they'd left their towels.

Alek kept himself more in line with the loaf-shaped kids, swimming decently, participating precisely as much as required. Natalie resented the coach for ratting out her son. It wouldn't have been a calamity if he had missed a few of these afternoons. The other boys, even Ned, seemed to know to leave Alek alone, like he was wounded.

On the drive home, Alek dead-ended every one of her questions.

The next day, after delivering him to the pool, she decided to forget about seemly. She went to the women's lockers and changed into her bathers. Diving into one of the open lanes

– a reasonable distance away from team practice – she saw that Alek hadn't even seen her. If he did, he looked unlikely to object.

Besides, she was aquatic. Her butterfly stroke threaded the water without a wake. Timing herself against the swiftest of the boys, she outdistanced all of them by laps. Even when they would take breaks or start skirmishes because they were tired, she found no need to stop. After the first twenty, she paused to check her pulse. It barely fluttered above its resting rate. She swam faster and farther than she ever had. And with more grace. This wouldn't be mentioned to Peter. It was too strange. If it continued for another week, she vowed to make an appointment with the GP. For the time being, she would enjoy it. She noticed the coach noticing her and, rather than have a conversation with him about it, slowed down to a human speed.

In the car, Natalie asked Alek why he wasn't talking to Ned.

"Not sure if I get him anymore."

"That's a shame. Did something happen between you two?"

"No."

"Did he do anything?"

"No."

"Did you do anything?"

"No." He grinned at an inside joke. "I don't do any-thing."

"What does that mean?"

"Nothing."

"You're being opaque."

Nothing.

Natalie waited a few minutes, commenting on the fiery leaves of an enormous maple – earning more of his sullen silence – before trying to connect again. "Vicenta hasn't been to dinner in a few weeks. Do you want to have her come by?"

"I'll ask her when I see her."

"Thursday would be good."

Alek put his fingers to his temples and said, "Let's ask her now."

His eyes rolled into a fixed position and stayed there for too long. Natalie tried to watch the road, but was alarmed at the intensity of his joke. He went utterly blank in the face. A few years back she'd had a student with epilepsy and had witnessed a seizure. This was how it began.

"Alek?"

He returned from wherever he had been. "What? I guess I'll invite her when I see her at school."

He drummed the window.

"Are you talking to anybody these days?" she asked.

"When I'm able to."

Another surge hit her: whatever was occupying his mind

was disrupting his education and his participation in the family. It was therefore her business. Forget the legitimacy of a boy child and his secrets. Any explanation he gave would have to be heard, but keeping a private life from your mother was an outrage against nature. If she had pulled to the side of the road and turned off the car, if she had pushed him against the passenger door, made him a little uncomfortable in order to get some answers, she would have screamed at him, one important word at a time, "This is real life!"

"Did you want to say something to me?" he asked.

It felt like a taunt. She let the fury subside. That was not the way to engender communication.

Calmly, she asked, "Do you still keep a diary at least? You were doing that at one point." A clang of guilt behind the question.

"Yes, I still keep a diary."

Which was more or less their last interaction until that night at dinner, when Sasha started to tease him about being driven around by his parents.

"No more disappearing acts, no more tricks, you'll have the toughest keepers in five towns. You're going to be living the clean life from now on—"

Peter, who had been betting from the start that drugs were the culprit, interrupted, "What do you mean a clean life?"

Sasha backtracked. "He doesn't need to be under lock and key. He just goes off into his head too much."

Alek exploded at all of them. "Is checking out every now and then some big sin? It's how I handle all of you. All right?" He left the table for the refuge of his room.

Sasha reached for his brother's remaining lamb. "Can I?"

Against the backdrop of Peter telling Sasha that he should be a kinder brother and the sound of Sasha scraping food onto his own dish, Natalie followed Alek upstairs. She knocked, but he said nothing. She knocked again, as if he would change his mind. The door was between them. What was she going to do? Break it down?

After dinner, she called her sister. Because Ruth was younger, because she had seen more, because she had lived through more, her solution would be more evolved than anything Natalie and Peter could devise. And Ruth enjoyed telling Natalie what she didn't want to hear.

Natalie broke through call waiting to find her on hold with the phone company. Ruth was trying to have the phone service turned on at the house she was moving into, the home that would finally, surely, help her feel centred. The word irritated. She conceded, though, that her sister's closer proximity would be a comfort.

Ruth instantly rattled off all the activities that might be stealing Alek's attention: girlfriends (other than the much-approved Vicenta), boyfriends, drugs, and petty crime. Or all of the above.

"Your prurience is appreciated," Natalie said.

"Or maybe he's selling – drugs and/or his body. It would show an entrepreneurial streak this family has lacked."

"That's hopeful. But what should I do?"

"At the end of the day, how far is he going to stray from the family purse? I say you're giving him exactly what he needs: space. He's got to answer his own questions."

"The school is asking their own questions and I don't have any answers. All I want to do is eviscerate him, if only to get some words out of him. Give me an angle here."

"Cover for him. Tell them he's very self-directed at the moment. He'll start next term in full flower."

"You don't even believe that."

"It's possible. What can I tell you? Give him the cold shoulder. Remember the silent treatment Giordana gave me? I matched her, glare for glare, for seven months. Neglected her thoroughly. I didn't have the time to do more than that. Look at her now: a firecracker. Plus, you've never been in love with that school. Give Alek at least as much credit as you're giving the staff there."

"I do, but he's become *not normal*."

"You would never have been satisfied with anything else. He's Alek. Do you think that you and Peter can handle the disgrace of not normal?"

"Yes."

"It happens. It will pass."

There. What she'd needed was perspective. "Thank you."

"Fabulous. Anything else to report?"

"Remember how I always wanted to be a terrific sleek swimmer? I've been in the pool a lot lately, and I have to say I'm going at it like a speedboat."

"Really? That's wonderful. I've been working two jobs to keep myself in shoes."

"I'm sorry. Do you need anything—?"

"Not a thing. Only your guilt."

"It's always here for you. Are Ben and Giordy all right?"

"They're finally off the payroll, so yes, they're fine."

"Anybody special worth mentioning?"

"No. But he'll fall into place after the move."

"I'm sure he will." This wasn't true.

"You're my favourite."

"You're mine." This was.

"Okay then hang up, so I can get back on hold."

That night, Natalie caught Alek in the hall and said to him, "I want to make a deal with you."

"What?"

"First, I have to make sure you're safe: do you need us to protect you from anybody or anything?"

"No. I can protect myself. I'm a grown-up."

Natalie said, "Exactly. That's why I want to treat you with the respect you deserve. From tomorrow, I'm not picking you up at school anymore. I'm not taking you to the pool. You don't want me to, so I won't. How's that?"

"What do I have to do?"

"Be worthy of it." She stared him down, as if to demand cooperation, before he retreated to his room. His eyes were only partly hazel, she realised. Not quite a single colour, but a palette – an expensive marble. She could have sworn she also saw a white flag floating in each of them.

Natalie lay across the bed, too warm to get under the covers. Peter was getting undressed. "Brutalising him won't help. We have to respect him," she said.

"So no more supervision?"

"I don't think there's much likelihood that it will benefit any of us."

Peter rubbed his whole face with his hand and yawned. "I'm sure you're as right as I am." And that was the end of it.

Natalie had been loving Peter in her terrified-of-losing-him way lately – more so, she had to admit, because of this acquiescence. After he showered, she waited for him, naked under the sheets. This was all she had to do to initiate.

He didn't last long. It had been a while and tomorrow was a work day. The closeness was appreciated. Afterwards, the sight of his depleted, sleeping soul, his skin already loosening its grip, underlined their difference. His few extra years seemed to matter more that night. Their marriage had surely slipped in certain areas. The thought didn't worry her. Natalie looked down at her own legs. They were tight along the contours of her muscles, like she had just been unwrapped.

Another fruitful day at school, with the children trailing her activity plan with such precision she could hear the switches clicking in their brains. In the afternoon, instead of harassing Alek, Natalie drove to the pond. When she got there it looked small, like a house you used to live in. Hardly worth it, so she circled back to the university. This was not, she insisted, an excuse to check up on him. She went for the outdoor pool, even parking by the science buildings so that the sight of the family station wagon wouldn't give him cause to complain.

In a lane by herself, she found that her speed had, impossibly, increased. The curve of her arms, the whirlpool created by her legs and the length of each breath felt more and more like she had been designed for the sea. This power didn't come from practise at the pond or from menopause. It was her body's antidote to Alek. She would be a lifeguard at the most dangerous beaches. *Baywatch* tough and mother soft. Shooting out to save one swimmer, then another, then another. She saw herself hauling a dozen near-lifeless bodies back to shore, turning them on their sides with factory efficiency and pumping them back to life, one after another.

When the university swimming team showed up for training, she dived under the separator and into the slow lane. There she swam around other women her age who were waiting for the water aerobics teacher to turn up. Natalie claimed the back edge of the pool and continued to do laps until their class was over. As if she were resting up after great exertion, she sat on the concrete lip, watching the water bead off her arms and wishing she could swim with the team.

As she left the car in the driveway, she could hear music coming from Sasha's room. No voices, only bass. Alek's runners were outside the front door, another recent weirdness. Still, the clues provided a pleasure: the boys were at home.

Letting herself in, she caught an unguarded glimpse of Alek. He was standing still at the back of the hallway. In the past, he would have been singing something, trailing his hands along the walls mindlessly as he went. When was the last time he'd made a voluntary sound?

His jacket and backpack were hanging off one shoulder. His pants were too long, and rumpled at his bare feet. If he stood up straight, he would be taller than she was, but that hadn't happened in a while. One would never know there was a beautiful boy under there.

Alek lurched when she finally shut the door behind her. There was a slight terror in his "hello," like he'd been caught. If she had confided to him her mysterious new energies, perhaps he would feel free enough to reveal something. No, it would still be coercion. We will both have our secrets, she accepted, as if that would be enough to keep the family together.

With all of her self-control, Natalie didn't search for signs of where he'd been. She kissed his cheek. A few days since it had seen a razor and still so soft. She consciously exhaled so as not to sniff for the scent of chlorine or alcohol or dope or Vicenta. Her conversation was restrained. She didn't provide any details of her day, which might be read as a lead-in to inquiries about his. She didn't offer to make his favourite pasta for dinner, as this might be construed as extortion. Instead, whenever she glanced in his direction, she simply gave him her warmest and most patient gaze, the one she reserved for her students who were closest to tears.

In return, he opened his backpack on the kitchen table, and did her the favour of lingering. Three textbooks came out, along with his copy of *Dune*, a dog-eared transitional object he'd been carrying around for months. This was followed by his empty lunch container and swimming gear. It was impossible to tell by looking if the dark green towel was damp. She made no offer to hang it up.

He had true promise when he was younger. Not merely bright, he had an ocean underneath him, an imagination that wasn't bound up with rules, a Byronic sensitivity that would one day develop into a melancholy but intelligent sweetness. Now the thought of his head filling up with the simplest facts – trucks and sports – would have satisfied her. At this point, she would have been content with average.

As she shuffled the day's mail, Alek opened one of his schoolbooks. Opening a letter, she paused to see what would happen next. For a hopeful moment it seemed as though he would do his homework at the table while she made dinner.

"May as well give the new wok a workout. What if I cut up some vegies for a stir-fry?" It was her most innocuous attempt, but talking wasn't in the deal. Alek packed up everything into a bundle and took it upstairs, leaving his empty lunch box on a chair.

At dinner, when Peter asked the boys about their day, Sasha regaled them with an account of the complications involved in selecting a mascot for the debating team. They had achieved a high standing in their division and were eager to find a way to shine at their own school in an otherwise athletic suburb. The team's most artistic member was barely able to draw a passable bear or fox – their preferred symbol. He could, however, draw a stunning mouse. For a team largely composed of boys who were not that physically impressive, this was a problem. Sasha bored them for the better part of the meal, discussing what changes were proposed to make the mouse more masculine.

It was never clear whether Sasha was truly eager for any of these activities or if he was, like Alek, getting away from the house. In any case, if they didn't all eat meals together on occasion, these reports wouldn't even reach Peter and Natalie. They were happy for any vestigial bursts of enthusiasm. Alek had never been as plugged in at school, but there was a time when he would have poked Sasha with a sharp question, laying bare the desperation of the whole mascot scheme. Natalie realised that Alek had stopped participating a while ago. Maybe Sasha's engagement was being provided as compensation.

Peter finally intruded, "And Alek, any news from your corner of the universe?"

"I attended school and swimming," he reported, as if he were having his activities notarised.

Sasha and Peter looked to Natalie to take charge. Again, angry energy coursed through her until she could gain control and allow it to erupt, soberly, as acceptance.

"I think we all have low days now and then."

Her face relaxed, serene after a glance at the three of them. A smile promised all would be well. Sasha and Peter, at least, were put at ease. She guided the conversation back to the debating team.

Watching and waiting was the path to take. Alek would eventually communicate. It wasn't confidence that allowed her to telegraph such inner peace. She had been thinking about the pool.

The week skimmed onwards in that unsustainable rhythm: Natalie powering her class all day, then racing laps faster than the swimming team; Peter accepting her wisdom without question; Alek holding himself hostage in his room except when leaving was mandatory. The topic of the unexplained absences vanished like lemon juice.

On Thursday Natalie came home from the pool to a quiet house. Upstairs there were no sounds from either of the boys' rooms. Hanging her bathers, goggles and towel in the laundry, she caught a view of her upper arms in the mirror. They looked streamlined, purpose-built for swimming. No wobble. It had been a while since she had studied her reflection. Even her curls looked tighter. She unbuttoned her blouse and unhooked her bra. She couldn't look at her body for long without thinking about Ruth's. Five years younger, practically identical, but diluted. She had more beauty and more warmth than Natalie, but had lost it on a series of poor choices. Wasted it. The latest was this move. She would be a twenty minute drive away, the closest they'd lived in years. How long would that last?

Ruth would have begged Natalie to pay more attention to her fantastic flush of power. She would tell her to swim constantly till she won medals, till she had only enough strength to make it out of the water and collapse onto the grass. She would tell Natalie that anything less was wasting it.

The lines of age around Natalie's neck and breasts had faded. The skin tone was even and clear. Her posture was forthright, her shoulders were muscled and her body was full. After forty-seven years of skinny, with far fewer curves than Ruth, she had expanded, desirably, to slim. She took up the right amount of space. What an unlikely development. Her face, when she finally caught her own eyes, was ready.

Natalie stole time from her routine to sit on the verandah. After Sasha was born, Peter had screened in the whole wooden frame to keep out mosquitoes and prevent him from crawling off the edge into the hydrangeas. Later, during the long afternoons of early motherhood, she would spread out the baby blanket on the floor. Sasha would toss blocks that Alek would fetch. And now: Sasha was conquering the world, one extra-curricular activity at a time; and perhaps Alek was on his way home with a brilliantly coherent explanation for everything.

A man shuffled around the corner and at first Natalie believed that the human droop was her son. It was an old man on a lonely walk through the neighbourhood. He smiled and waved. Natalie did the same and thanked God he wasn't Alek. One morning, a decade earlier, while she had been sitting in the same spot watching over the boys, Alek suddenly went to war with a table and used both hands to push it over. Barely missing Sasha's head, it tore a gash in the wall. Like a prisoner working on his tunnel, Alek started picking at the hole and, after Peter repaired it, the patch. Escape had become more engaging than his big brother.

Even when they shared a room, they had never been close. This, despite all the thoughtful timing for them to be close in years and, thus, in spirit. There had also been Peter's hopeful dream, pulling both of their names from one of his long dead grandfathers, Aleksander. Their namesake had been a farmer in a Russian village so tiny and then so obliterated that it was lost to maps. How could he have dreamt up these irrelevant descendants with their reflective runners and thumping music? Peter had hoped that curiosity would lead the boys to learn Russian and travel, or work for the United Nations. For what reason? "For the sake of the past," he had said. The boys didn't know about the homeland, didn't like Peter's mother's stuffed cabbage when Natalie tried to make it, and everyone in Russia was busy learning English. *Perestroika*, the world couldn't help itself, it was always being rebuilt.

The phone rang. It was the assistant principal. "Alek didn't come to school today. I think we ought to plan for a meeting here, so that we can attempt to figure out what's actually going on."

Natalie could have lifted a car. While she was absorbing this news, Alek walked up the street. It was a relief at least to see that he was spryer than the old man who had passed by earlier. She let her side of the phone conversation lapse into one-word responses as he came into the house. A peace-making open hand was all he gave her, half of a high five. If she had put her hand up to meet it, he would have shied away. He headed up to his room as she let a meeting be scheduled for next week.

"Thank you," she told the assistant principal and put down the phone.

She soared after him, barely feeling her feet on the stairs. It became a scene immediately, with her pushing on one side of his door, and him pushing back from the other.

"That was the school. I trusted you."

"I don't care. I don't want to talk about it."

"You have to tell me what's going on," she said.

"I don't have to do anything!"

"Please, I'm on your side." She used more of her force against the door.

"You're not. You're on my back."

This was how she could be a good mother: there was a basic parental obligation to make sure he was safe. Starting now, Natalie would stop trying to protect him from herself. She slammed right in, bashing the door against the wall, leaving a mark in the plaster. He backed against the window, small and shrinking, till he had slumped below the frame.

Natalie followed him down, holding him by the front of his shirt. There had never been a tussle like this in the house before. Alek had a slight smile on his face, as if this was what he'd wanted her to do all along. She shook him to let him know she was very serious.

"Talking will, at the very minimum, get us off your back. Speak."

Less than a breath away, she watched his face. He seemed to be reaching for and finding what he needed to say. Thoughts sprouted and his readiness for the confrontation seemed even stronger. He looked almost game, beginning to inhabit himself, becoming larger as he sorted out his words. The confession, whatever it was, was winding together into sentences that would clarify. All would be forgiven and understood. Natalie relaxed her grip and sat back on her knees so he could compose himself from a less vulnerable stance. There was a fresh intake of air, as if he was about to commence with a clear statement of self. She was ready to receive. Then, as if it had all grown too thick too quickly, his face faltered. He could no longer verbalise it. Even if he could, she wouldn't understand. The sentences were too long, the explanation was too complicated. It was beyond either of them. She saw all of this in his shaking expression. He shuddered and gave up. It had been close, but at the last minute he had failed. He dissolved into the helplessness of crying.

Her pulse slackened. This wasn't a sadness she could touch. Out of deference to it, she left him there on the floor.

Peter was late coming home, so she couldn't find enough time before dinner to sit him down and tell him about Alek. Sasha had a band meeting in the next town, which meant that the meal itself would leave the three of them alone.

To questions about his week, Alek gave answers that were wordy enough to satisfy Peter and false enough to make Natalie uncomfortable.

After they had finished the dishes, she told Peter about the assistant principal but not the stand-off upstairs. It was bad enough that he had taken advantage of her trust. She couldn't admit to having used force – unsuccessfully – on their teenaged son. Already, Alek was beginning to feel like her fault.

"What should we do now?" Peter asked, without even a touch of blame. Natalie was grateful, but still didn't have an answer. How would they undo whatever it was they had done in order to get him to speak again?

"I don't know," she said.

Peter shrugged sympathetically and left the matter with her.

When he climbed into bed next to her, she curled slowly, as if already asleep, towards him, showing enough affection for a cuddle but not enough energy to discuss their son any more. Falling into a light sleep, it occurred to her that the mastery of parenthood was learning to care less and less.

At 4 a.m., Natalie stole away from Peter's snoring and his warmth, and out to the carpeted silence of the hall. No driving energy or concern woke her. She was simply awake again, watching over everyone. Sasha's light was off and his bed was empty. Alek's door was closed, but the light was on. The sound of conversation came from inside.

Natalie wanted to knock. They would open it and let her in. It would be a midnight clubhouse, like when the boys used to commandeer the backyard for the afternoon and invite Peter and Natalie to watch plays that usually revolved around juvenile puns.

They had graduated to adolescent secrets, which explained the closed door. Sasha had reached him and tonight Alek was talking. She would listen and show matter-of-factness about any transgression he threw at her. The only necessary ingredient was his tiny faith in her capacity to hear it, but surely she had earned it by now.

As Sasha would say: *as if.*

Natalie lowered herself to look through the keyhole.

Alek, in grey tracksuit pants and a grey hoodie, was sitting on the edge of his unmade bed alone. No sign of Sasha. On his lap, Alek was holding the diary open. He was looking at an architectural drawing of an elephant hanging on the wall, some poster he had brought back from a school trip to a science museum when he was eleven. Recently, he had asked Peter to frame it. The frame had to have a gold finish, it had to be shiny. Alek had been particular and Peter had been feeling indulgent.

Alek spoke with reverence in the general direction of the elephant and smiled – more pleasantly than he had at any of them in weeks. It looked like he was also listening, as if the elephant were explaining an extremely detailed plan.

Where was Sasha? Now she remembered him saying he would be sleeping over with one of the boys from the debating team.

Alek stood up and walked over to the wall, placing his ear near the elephant's mouth. A slow nod indicated comprehension, followed by a little laugh. His eyes looked half-dead, like they did when he went into that daze in the car. He vacantly smiled at the wall. This wasn't part of any school play. This wasn't an imaginary friend.

He nodded again, then faced the page of the diary,

which she knew was as blank as his face. His head bobbed, as if he was taking dictation, his index finger tracing words around the paper and weaving with occasional flourishes. Then he turned a page and continued. When he spoke, his voice was too quiet and rushed to make out what he was saying, but he addressed the elephant for about a minute. Not troubled – confiding, the way he used to talk to Ned. At some point, his gaze changed. Whatever the situation had been, it was over. Alek laid the shoelace across the diary, and then closed it, adjusting the book in the centre of his lap with a look of satisfaction. The day's thoughts had been recorded and he was a good boy. But she didn't recognise him. He was somebody else's good boy, not hers.

Alek hugged his pillow and continued talking with variations – softly here, an angry edge there, sometimes waiting for a response that she couldn't hear. At the end he was silent, but he turned his eyes to the ceiling, his neck jutting forwards as if he was listening to the scratching of mice.

This happened to boys his age.

An involuntary "Oh," escaped from her lips and she pulled away from the door. When she peered back in she saw that he hadn't even flinched. This was what was going on. This was why he had closed them all off.

Natalie was no longer the author of her family. How she would handle the assistant principal, how she would talk to Alek from now on – that was the least of it. There was no more hoping that the right words from her or Vicenta or Ned or Sasha would make him the way he was last year, or two years ago. When was it he had last been a regular kid? Ever?

In the hall she could hear the house settling into the chill. If four in the afternoon was the most feverish hour for the sick body, four in the morning should be the coolest, but here was Alek, so politely and thoroughly disturbed.

Within a few minutes, Natalie was driving through their neighbourhood. The order of it all was striking, as if maintaining appearances required no effort. The rubbish at the kerb awaiting collection, the joggers on the road before six, the quiet, empty high school looking forward to inhaling all the children of the town except Alek.

The note she left in the kitchen said she was leaving for work early. No one would find it for at least another hour. The message she left at school was that she had a stomach bug and wasn't coming in.

The highway to the beach wasn't busy yet, so she darted her way through truckers and long-distance commuters. The drive would take time and she would likely be caught in some tie-up along the way. It didn't matter.

Every radio station was broadcasting something trivial. There was no recognisable music at this hour. She tried to whistle or sing but didn't have the ability to sustain anything against the flow of her thoughts and all the people who were, for the morning, behind her.

There was a particular beach she had in mind. It had high dunes and a real surf. They had been there a few times as a family. Only when she was approaching its strip of motels did Natalie remember that the last time they were there a wave dumped Alek so hard that Peter had to carry him, in tears, up to the lifeguard station. He had cuts all over his chest and took an hour to settle down, glaring at the seas as if it had done it on purpose. All the more reason to swim here. He had spent the rest of that afternoon out past the sandy stretch of the beach, fascinated by the busy little worlds of rocky tide pools.

"They're so delicate," Alek said. "A big wave comes by and shakes it all up like an Etch A Sketch and it has to start all over again."

He would make a wonderful marine biologist, she thought at the time. All he had to do was get back in the water.

When she pulled into the car park, a group of surfers were already finishing, drying off by a station wagon. Natalie parked a distance from them, close to the beach and the empty lifeguard chair. She changed in the front seat and walked down to the sand as the sun turned the morning water to gunmetal.

In the protected corner of a dune, four teenage boys were huddled under blankets, sitting around a dead bonfire from the night before. There were beer bottles planted in the sand all around them and they were laughing loud enough to be heard over the surf. Healthy, sane.

No one else was in the water. The waves were breaking close to the shore, loudly, with a pace that would be hard to interrupt. Natalie hadn't tried her new skill in the ocean, but she was unafraid. She put on her goggles and dived through the whiteness. The cold forced air from her lungs, but she managed to jump through the waves to less turbulent water. In a minute she couldn't touch the bottom and the temperature dropped. But it was tolerable. If she remembered her landmarks and followed the coastline at this distance, she could swim for as long as she wanted.

Straightening her course on the water, she began. The tide lifted her as she swam with the line of the waves. *If I swim far enough...* That was the feeling that had brought her here. There was no end to the sentence. If. As though some deal had to be struck.

Eventually she would go home, tell Peter, call the school, and turn Alek over to a chorus of professionals who would pretend to know what he needed. They would all get sucked up in a sad circle of hopes and failures.

When she looked back and saw that the dunes had given way to a rockier coastline, she turned away from land, and headed straight out. The ocean was endless, but she knew it wouldn't drown her.

This is what it's like where he's going.

She pushed through to the next swell.

Where we're going.

The thought already felt like a cure.

If.

With her arms and legs making tiny nicks in the surface of the ocean, she still might be able to rescue him. All she had to do was concentrate on swimming faster than him, swimming all the way to Russia if she had to, and surely she would have the strength to bring him back.

Ben

He had spent nearly three hours trying to get the sparrow out of the apartment. Despite the need for air conditioning against the heat, he usually propped a window open with a brick to keep things circulating. It was the only open window on the block and that's how the bird got in in the first place.

A second before Janelle slipped her key in the front door, the sparrow, as if sensing that the available fun was about to be sucked from the situation, escaped. Up till then the bird hadn't been in a particular rush. On its way out, it managed to tear a snag across two muslin curtains before swooping out to freedom. It perched on the fire escape, for one last look at the lumpy and confused guy, sticking his head out of the window, and took off. There was a smile on the sparrow's tiny beak. It was delighted.

Then Janelle was home. 7.30 p.m. and she was expecting dinner and a sleeping toddler. Instead, there was no sign of food and the apartment looked ransacked. The chase had left its mark on every surface. The punchbowl was in five useless pieces on the kitchen floor. The entire legacy of Ben's father, and they used it for fruit. No fruit was visible, only shards, making it clear that the shopping hadn't even been done. Janelle steadied a stern glance at Ben's tracksuit pants, the ones he lived in, as if to ask if he had even broken a sweat that day.

The fact of the sparrow's invasion carried no weight with Janelle at all. What was the justification for the open window anyway? If she had asked, Ben was prepared to say that this might have happened on any day in any other season when one opens a window. But it happened today, Janelle would say, and he would hate her for the adolescent logic.

Ivan was roaming around the sofa and making noises about the prolonged bird chase.

When it was just Ben and Janelle they had done well. They had been so young it was like a head start in front of everyone else. Janelle planned and Ben implemented. They saved, they travelled. There was time to be cheerful. Her career went one way, his went the other – they adjusted. Since Ivan, though? Ben didn't like to blame an innocent kid who had never asked to be born… but.

As Ben cleaned up the aftermath of the chase, he desperately recounted for Janelle the lame strategies he had wasted hours on, with broom, with bucket, with album cover – each of which the bird seemed to comprehend with a superior intelligence and respond to with an even more superior attitude. It would wait him out in some hidden nook, then race across the room, studiously avoiding all the open windows, to find another as-yet unwrecked corner of the small apartment. What Ben was trying to relate was that it was so frustrating it was funny. The point he ended up making, though, was that the sparrow won.

Ben hurried to heat a frozen block of stew into a presentable dinner. Janelle used the time to wind Ivan down, rocking him against her shoulder as he slowly wheezed himself quiet. Ben noticed she still had her house keys in one hand, as if retaining the right to walk out and find a different home and husband for the night.

"Ivan needs a new nappy," she said.

"Anything else?" he asked from the kitchen.

Whatever other improvements she could imagine in their life, she kept them to herself.

The stew was still cold in the centre. Ben watched Janelle survey the remains of their living room. The deep scratch on the dining room table. The tear in the sofa cushion. He didn't even know how that one happened.

"Must have been a vicious sparrow. It looks like the leather was cut with a knife," she said.

Janelle untangled a piece of elbow pasta from her son's hair.

She couldn't help but say it out loud: "It's so ridiculously emblematic."

The next morning was all about finding a repair shop for the cushion. Janelle loved that sofa and fixing it would serve as penance. After all, he was the one with the free schedule. On the phone, a man told Ben that it was possible to mend it. Despite Ivan's refusal to sit still in his stroller and his penchant for public tantrums, the prospect of being able to present an affordable solution to Janelle remained a priority for Ben in planning the day. Ivan struggled like a strapped demon for the train ride. Two minutes before they arrived at their stop and in front of an unimpressed mid-morning commuter audience, he threw up all over Ben's runners. A few baby wipes were sacrificed for the clean up as Ivan's tears started again.

"Hope you enjoyed the show," Ben muttered to the crowd, wheeling Ivan from the train.

Giordana often told Ben how awed she was with his stay-at-home status. She said, "Your son will teach you everything you need to know about the universe." Maybe she was being ironic when she said it. While Ben was sponging Ivan's body fluids from various places, she had nearly finished her PhD. And she wasn't showing any sort of pull towards breeding either. Her frequent declaration that she was happily single used to seem like a twisted delusion. Ben now saw it as wisdom.

The shop where he was going to have the cushion repaired specialised in fetish gear. At the counter, a man in a leather police cap took a disapproving look at the cushion and said,

"Not that leather. I don't have the needle." Ivan was waving his hand back and forth through a curtain of whips. Ben placed the cushion in the stroller and kept the boy close beside him as they left the shop.

It was still early. At least they'd get some exercise. After the struggle of applying sunscreen to Ivan's flinching face, Ben led them home along the waterfront, stopping every few steps to let his son point out a passing truck or pick up a cigarette butt. At some unguarded moment, Ivan managed to pry open the sippy cup he had been fondling all morning and spill grape juice onto the cushion's wound. Ben dabbed it off without losing his temper, even as the slit turned a permanent purple. From now on, the cushion would simply be turned over. *That is,* he thought, *so ridiculously emblematic.*

Negotiating the boy through a steady current of barely dressed joggers and bike riders, Ben felt more ungraceful than ever. He was bogged by the foolishness of wheeling a stained cushion around, by Ivan wandering in all directions, and by his very own flesh. Would things have been that much different if he had a job? In her mind they would.

For lunch, he gave up on getting Ivan to eat anything nutritious and sat on a bench, letting the boy feed him peeled carrot sticks one by one from a plastic bag. Ivan fed him the celery sticks next. After that, Ben let him eat a completely unearned vanilla pudding on his own.

They watched a hovering group of gulls dip and bounce

above the water, gently rocking like the small waves below them. Ben thought of a mobile and tried to teach Ivan the word. He explained it as different pieces of art on different branches, like a tree, but balancing each other and hanging from the ceiling, and staying still or spinning, depending on the breeze. Ivan repeated the word back to him, but couldn't have understood. The boy wasn't as verbal as they would have liked. This was also presumed to be Ben's doing, since he was home with him all day. Ivan handed the cushion to his father as he climbed into the stroller and sat down, kicking his legs for them to go.

Ben pushed onwards to the park, commending himself for saving the cost of the train. He headed to a favourite bench in a secluded corner. It was shut off from the main field by a small ridge of climbable rocks and a solitary tree that shaded the whole area – landscaped for a child's enjoyment and a parent's watchful eye.

But Ivan was contentedly snoring in the shade. He wasn't about to climb anything. The boy already looked chunky from a steady diet of Cheerios, pasta and inaction. This was Ben's contribution too. Why not teach him about the joys of beer this afternoon? Get him started early. Ivan was probably doomed to a lifetime of slept-through opportunities and unhealthy sloth. Ben planned to let him go on napping for twenty minutes and then wake him so that he would, A, be able to sleep later, and B, (although Ben wasn't actually in the mood) play spaceman on the rocks. This bit of exertion would fortify Ivan for all the setbacks to come. Ben could hope.

A bird interrupted.

A large, brown, hawk-like creature walked sternly across the patchy grass towards the bench. It staked out the highest rock, all the while keeping a curious gaze on Ben and Ivan. It had a butcher's knife beak and a steely expression, as if it knew what the sparrow had gotten away with and was about to commence an even more destructive plan of action.

The bird opened its wings out slowly, purposefully, and with a push, launched itself upwards, leaping to a higher perch in the tree. The branch swayed with the new weight. The bird paused, keeping its wings spread, showing off the same move a few more times as it made its way up and up. At each stop it tilted its head at him kindly with the allure of someone demonstrating a salad slicer, as if to say, *See? You can do this too*. Finally, it pushed off and out into the sky, without looking back.

Surely this made up for the attitude of that sparrow.

What the hell? For his own exercise, Ben stood up and climbed to the bird's spot on the top of the rock. Panting from the ten steps, he held his arms out to the sun and that felt good enough. King of the city, top of the world. Pathetic. At least no one was looking. He listed back and forth on his ankles in the sun. He hopped up once to amuse himself. The first jump felt higher than the push that caused it. He concentrated on imitating the bird's movements, and hopped again, this time with more force, and went up, staying there without gravity, for what felt like three seconds. It was strangely high for a jump. He did it again and found that if he flexed his elbows behind him he could steer more easily on the way back down to the rock.

Steer?

Ivan would have commanded him, "Again."

Ben jumped again, using all of his power. His body met the wind in an equal embrace. He was wrapped in it and sliding upwards in a slender curve, almost as high as the first branch of the tree. His arms knew exactly where to go to keep control. He guided himself slowly down, his feet coming to rest next to the stroller. Ivan was still sleeping with a worried scowl. Poor kid, decades of scowls awaited. Ben relaxed his knees in a slight dip, raised his arms over his head dramatically, like a violinist spiralling towards a crescendo, and soared up.

Instantly he was above the tree, balancing the wind long enough to gain his bearings. He remembered the gulls they saw earlier and admired them for making these mechanics look so effortless. Once he was in motion he felt more in control, so he thrust up and then down, circling their private corner of the park in jags.

He felt light.

Slowly, the details became recognisable. At first there was a dull geometry to the view. From above, people and trees were reduced to circles of hair or hats. Cars, in all their costly variations, were levelled into equivalent rectangles. Winding paths were brief and only for show, stopping at the park's boundaries. Streets crossed avenues and made up the ungraceful grid. The rooftops, just drab squares from here, told nothing of the grandeur beneath. It was like seeing a beautiful painting from the side.

But that was only when he looked down. The older buildings that stood along the edge of the park had been carved, corniced and gargoyled for optimum fourth-floor viewing. He shot up and the ragged skyline belonged entirely to him. Beyond that, if he pushed a bit more, he was able to see the river and the city sprawl beyond.

Birds drifted by in the distance, floating on the same breeze. Did they even appreciate the view? He watched them as he experimented with his manoeuvres, expecting them to welcome him to their tribe. They would explain all their tricks and lead him to their favourite haunts. But even when he briefly stumbled, losing altitude in a clumsy twist, they didn't seem to notice. It didn't matter; he would pretend to be relaxed about the whole thing too. He didn't want to look like an amateur.

The airy afternoon light was a few shades brighter up here and, as a new inhabitant, he observed a different dimension: there was sky beneath him. Sky was no longer limited to up.

On the verge of waking, Ivan stretched in his seat, pushing his empty sippy cup to the ground. The sound it made knocked up through the wind till it found Ben. Before

Ivan could even begin to whimper, his father dove down, inventing a flourish as he spiralled once around the tree and landed. Not entirely awake, Ivan saw his father lower smoothly into view. With a smile, Ben picked up the cup and tucked it back into his son's sticky hands.

"Watch: when I tell your mother, she'll say I'm doing it wrong."

Ivan giggled and yawned. He stuck his finger up to get his father to give another performance, but Ben whisked him away from the bench before he had the chance to wonder why he hadn't been taken out of the stroller to play.

At the market Ben splurged and bought salmon, Janelle's favourite, for reasons of nutrition and brain vitamins. He would soften her up. That evening, she came home to a clean house and a calm child. As they ate dinner, she expressed her thanks. So far, so good. After, he would show her what else he could do.

Janelle watched as he fed Ivan. A spoonful of peas dropped down the front of the bib, but Ben wasn't fast enough to catch them all. "Watch him," she said. The tone had made an appearance.

The week before, Alek had invited himself to dinner and managed to scatter his own food everywhere and spill his wine, but Janelle was able to laugh it off. As she tossed him the sweep-up sponge, she pretended to be carefree about the whole thing. Alek kept on talking, entertaining Ivan with his general weirdness, the sponge unused in his hand. All the patience and mercy of the family had gone to Alek. Ben didn't get a drop.

The night that Alek had visited, when Ivan saw what Alek could get away with, he flung a potato at the floor and looked around, waiting for applause. Alek and Ben couldn't help but smile.

"Don't do that," Janelle had said and all of them went quiet. Who was in trouble this time? Ben reflexively picked up the errant potato. Even Alek, not always the most clear-eyed and observant, looked at Ben with sympathy.

Tonight, Ben's response was to ignore both the peas and the tone in favour of more important matters. Janelle glanced under the highchair.

"They're waiting to be stepped on," she said.

"They're peas. They'll have to be patient." He was already losing wood for this.

"And what else happened today?" she asked, making a sudden bid for rapport.

This was the moment. Where to begin? The hawk, the city, the weightlessness? How could he sell it to her?

His pause was too long. The delay was proof that he had done nothing.

"It seems bizarre to me, not being able to account for it. I know what I did today. I went to work. Have you sent out one letter this week?" She was already curating a different evening. The discussion would be his dim connections to his vaporised career as a lab researcher. Janelle had always politely pretended they held more promise than they did. The opportunities withered as he sought increasingly peripheral jobs, to the point that a twenty-year-old secretarial student would have been more affordable and more attractive. There had been talk about retraining, but that had receded, as his days were full of Ivan. The letters she was always talking about would be for glorified cleaning positions at other people's labs. They would, as Janelle never tired of pointing out, still be jobs, as if work were an end in itself. Keeping Ivan out of day care, being frugal with the family budget – that never figured into her accounting.

"What happens to your time?" she asked as if she were truly curious. There was no telling her anything.

Ivan decided to toss a handful of peas at her. Again, Ben couldn't help but be impressed by the kid's sense of timing. He smiled.

"Please Ben. Don't make me into this person."

"I haven't spoken."

Janelle exhaled and stood up to bring her dish to the kitchen.

"Leave it. I'll do them," he told her.

This was the unlovely deal that they had ended up with.

That night Ben dreamt about the moon landing. He woke up and the room was dark, except for the light over Janelle's side. He didn't remember details – only the footage of his first slow step onto its sugary surface.

Janelle was turned towards the window, still reading under the dome of her light. He knew that she knew that he was awake, even though neither of them had moved or spoken. The book she was reading was about how to find perfect peace in the everyday. Making headway? She was still, for better and for worse, his best friend. She was the wisest person he knew. She made their money. When she was fully at ease, between 2 p.m. and 4 p.m. on a Saturday, they could make each other happy. When she had the time and energy, she was even an indulgent mother.

Ben stretched back, nudging her shoulder. She didn't acknowledge him. He imagined harmony spinning over their bed, always out of reach. They weren't alone. It was above every couple, every night. He looked past Janelle's book to the open bedroom door that let them share their air conditioning with Ivan across the hall. Was their imperfect peace blowing over his innocent body? Was it being inhaled?

The next day Ben called Alek to look after Ivan. He had offered to babysit a dozen times before but Janelle always squinted at the prospect. Ivan was too precious, too absorptive to be left alone in his care. Never mind. Alek was available and he was there in half an hour. He was embarrassingly grateful for the chance and patiently listened to the many instructions that came with looking after a two-year-old.

Ben went back to the same rock and it still worked. At first he worried some official entity would shoot him down. He quickly figured out how to punctuate his meanderings with vertical swoops, so that his shape would remain indistinct to anyone below. He also learned how to go faster – as if he were dashing from one spot to the next. All was still, gravity was less demanding, and there were no people or cars to fight as he crossed the city. Loops and turns and approaches became easier. He began to understand how air worked.

By the afternoon, he'd grown bored with the tourist spots. He started to go deeper, lingering over private back-yards and hidden alleys where he could see what people did when they thought they weren't being watched. Unsurprisingly, they cried to themselves, they had sex, they stared into space. They read with oblivion, they looked around waiting to be noticed. Sometimes, when they were doing simple things, like pouring water from a jug, he saw loneliness in the gesture, as if they would rather be pouring it for other people too. All of this was profoundly moving. It was absolutely wasted on birds. In fact, he was surprised to find himself less, rather than more, attuned to birds in general. They took this great picture for granted. The human suffering he witnessed ought to be archived. He'd make a documentary about the real workings of the streets, the city in all its emotional chaos. He'd keep a record – for somebody. Who? Father Christmas? The instinct was to report it to Janelle. If he could fly through not only space but time, he would go back five years so she would actually listen to him. Now she would only care if he could make his enterprise profitable. With more control than a helicopter, he might become a traffic reporter. Amazing? No. His plan was to keep wandering the sky. Another one of his aimless journeys.

A different angle: what if all anyone needed in order to do this was take the right lessons? He could become Instructor Number One and share his knowledge with other men like himself. An army of househusbands taking to the skies. What an excellent excuse they would all have for not doing the laundry.

To test this theory, he headed to a neighbourhood near the water, where he didn't normally go. Three drag queens were leaning against a building. Surely they would have the imagination to give it a shot. He offered to show them a way to punch up their acts. They offered him a makeover.

"First this," he said, standing up on a crate. He remembered not to slouch, not in order to improve his take-off, but to make him look more professorial. His students fell into position next to him, hands on hips like they were learning the macarena. If he could teach them, they would become his followers. The one in the hotpants would make an especially effective advertisement for his service and for the city itself. Picture the tourist billboards.

Ben started with the basic jumps, allowing the slightest excess in his leap so as not to excite them too much. In their heels they could barely get off the street. He made them try barefoot and from a few other positions, but they came up only as high as mortals. He thought moving directly to arm movements would be the way to go, but they laughed, thanked him for playing, and went back to holding up the building. The one in the hotpants offered him a hit of vodka, which he declined.

"You sure? You look like you could use a pick-me-up."

Ben shook his head and walked the length of the street. Once he could look back and see the three of them gabbing, dissecting the experience and, probably, him as well, he took off, sailing past their open mouths.

Back at home Alek was exuberant, almost florid. Ivan had apparently provided him with a breakthrough and Alek's face was alive with revelation as he reported what had happened. That morning, Ben had left strict orders that Ivan could only leave the house in big boy's underpants if he had been to the toilet. Otherwise, it was nappies. This had been a contentious issue for the last few weeks and the addition of a novice apparently raised the stakes. When it had come time to leave, Ivan swore he didn't have to go to the bathroom and similarly swore that he wouldn't put on a nappy. They wound up in a fierce battle at the changing table, with Ivan shrieking that he wanted to wear big boy's underpants and Alek trying desperately to wrap him in a nappy. At the tantrum's crisis point, Ivan dictated that he would settle only if he could wear both, the big boy underpants and the nappy.

"And I let him!" Alek said, as if he'd just unfolded the universe.

Ivan pulled down his pants to display their lumpy teamwork. He stood proud, with his jeans below his dimpled knees.

Ben snorted. "Don't show your mother."

Alek pointed proudly at Ivan the Littlest Genius. "This is everything, right here. All of our possibilities, in one little boy."

"Right." Alek was crazy. You could probably see it from space.

"You're not getting it. Ivan found the words he needed to get what he wanted. He's better than we are. Smarter than me, an adult and still at home with my parents. Smarter than you and Janelle in your miserable marriage."

Ivan stared up at Alek, a finger holding onto the elastic of his pants.

"Thanks," Ben said.

"Think about it. We haven't asked for what we want yet. Right now, we're in the wrong version of our lives. Too much security, too little freedom. That was Ivan's problem and he found a way out. So can we. All we have to do is pick a different story, one where we get what we want. That's where you and I will see each other next." It sounded nice, choosing another channel like that. *In this version, I'll have wings.*

Alek kissed Ben on his forehead, chin and both cheeks. "Your boy is so wonderful."

Ben considered telling him about his afternoon above the city, but he didn't think Alek could have handled any additional amazement.

Ben brought the depressed in from ledges; he found lost children and led them to their parents; he retrieved cats, kites and frisbees. An old woman slipped him a twenty for untangling her grandson's balloon from a tree. When he brought a bottle of water to an old man changing a tyre by the side of the highway in the hottest part of the afternoon, Ben heard, for the first time in his life, somebody call him a hero. His mother's voice: *that word gives you reason to reflect, doesn't it?*

He floated above the city, considering it. I could go away, he thought. Leave Janelle and Ivan and go and do this instead. What Alek had said even made some sense. Say goodbye to security and be free to serve. It sounded noble. He wasn't too old. The security part might turn up again, elsewhere. In the meantime, he could avoid a future of professional malaise and arguments about peas. There was a way for him to contribute to the good of the world; there were people who needed him. And Janelle could spend the rest of her days berating this deadbeat Superman who'd abandoned her. Who was he fooling? He wasn't the type to seize such a chance. That, as Janelle would have said, was the entire problem.

Publicity would have helped. Not that he cared, but the next time she asked what happened to his days it would be devastating if he could present her with a dramatic visual, proof that he was good for more than chores.

He set out to get some press. The goal was small items, one-paragraph reports, preferably with a photograph. In films, tights or a cape were expected but he was sure the effect wouldn't be as appealing on him. He wore his interview suit, minus the vest. He got a haircut and sculpted his sideburns. The aim was to get the word 'stylish' in front of 'hero'.

He became bolder in his excursions, showing up to assist at house fires and car accidents. Someone or something always needed to be saved. He chose larger groups, scanning for people with cameras, sometimes even posing with his arms spread open as he landed, maintaining a face of beneficence, as if he were an angel. The ones who witnessed his descent inevitably flocked to him, asking questions. He was coy about giving his name, fearing he would end up in some remote government lab. "I'm going to go help" became his excuse for leaving quickly. The phrase left a bit to be desired as a tagline, but it never became an issue. They told no one, certainly none of the major news outlets. Or he was reading the wrong papers.

At home, at least, Janelle appreciated his new fastidiousness. Ivan was happier, largely because the sitter he had employed instead of Alek allowed him to play all day in the sandpit while she sat on a nearby bench breaking up and reuniting with her boyfriend over the phone. The most tangible change was that Ben had started to lose weight. One day Janelle even commented on it.

"I've been doing a lot of walking," he told her.

As soon as he said it, he panicked that he was telling the truth. Was this all imagined? Was he any saner than Alek? Yes. What he was experiencing was too vivid. Wasn't it?

The next day, he strapped his son to his chest in one of his old carriers. The boy, wiggling as always, faced forward as they headed into the park. To lighten things for the long journey, Ben found a shady spot and stowed his shoes and socks under a bush. He put on his Ray-Ban goggles, rocked back and forth, and took off.

Hovering a few feet from the ground, he asked Ivan what he thought.

"Up," the boy said, squirming. He was proud that his son had the spirit of excitement.

Ben moved cautiously, circling up around the thick trunk of a tree, keeping one hand on Ivan's chest until he had fully integrated the effect of the added load. Ben put both arms straight out and extended his back so that he could take them up above the street, above the trees and to the river. Over the water, Ben found the gust he expected and turned into it.

The weight on his chest made flight awkward. He felt like a fish swimming up an endless staircase. Finally, he reached a navigable layer that could support them. Stretching his arms in front to reduce shear, and putting his feet behind him like a rudder, he tucked his head between his arms and sped forwards.

From time to time, he looked down at Ivan. The boy held his arms straight out in faithful imitation. When Ben's body tilted or dipped, he didn't fight it. He mimicked his father's every move, probably wondering why he'd never been taken here before. They brushed against a cloud and Ivan tried to shake the droplets from his face. They passed a flock of geese and Ivan waved at them briefly, but then put his arm back in place, keeping his body in line with his father's.

A steady string of spit slid from his amazed mouth. It was a struggle for him to keep his eyes open in the wind. If Ben were truly switched-on, he would have brought goggles for Ivan and jackets for both of them.

From above, their destination was easy to find. The top of the stately brick-red dome stuck out of the hillside when they were still a good ten minutes away. He pushed on through the wind, shifting downwards to capture some of the earth's warmth. There was the circuit that earthlings were restricted to: the highway to the bridge to the local road; the roundabout where you forked left after the reservoir; and the maze of smaller roads that took you to the hotel's long driveway. Ben followed a straight line over it all. There were no missed exits when you travelled like this – no blind turns, no traffic. From above, the unity of all places was clear – this highway connected to that road, this part of the forest tilted away from that part of the forest in a softer green. Why couldn't he live his life from such an angle?

The broad verandah would have been the logical place to set down, but guests were sitting on rockers, staring wistfully out at the lawn, and at least one navy-shirted staff member was visible. This was not the kind of establishment where he wanted to stage a photo op. It wasn't fair. Birds could do what they wanted without anyone asking them questions.

The lawn around the hotel was dotted with patrons.

There was a family croquet game going on and some boys in matching lime polo shirts, collars up, playing miniature golf by a stream. Poseurs. Ben found a gap in a nearby hedge, a respectable distance away from other guests. It was suitable for landing. He unharnessed Ivan and the boy collapsed on the ground in a happy heap, still damp and shivering from the cold. He threw his arms in the air – not to be picked up, but to remember the feeling. He looked up at Ben with drunken awe as they warmed themselves on the lawn.

The concierge gave the faintest nod as the barefoot man led his son through the panelled lobby towards the stairs. Ivan ran ahead to the second floor balcony.

When Ben caught up, the boy was telling an old man in a linen suit, "I bird Daddy."

"You birded your Daddy?"

Ivan put his arms out in front of him. The man put his arms out too. Ivan nodded up at him earnestly. Ben was temporarily grateful that his son's verbal skills weren't in the higher percentiles.

Ben sweetly waved his arms too, smiling at the old man as he pushed his son back into the corridor.

"I bird," Ivan shrieked at anyone walking by.

Ben couldn't help himself. "Maybe some day Ivan bird, but today Daddy bird."

Ivan pouted. "No. Ivan bird."

"No. Daddy bird."

Ben pulled Ivan into a stairwell and, with no breeze,

performed a small loop up to the floor above and back down. He landed in front of Ivan. "Okay, your turn."

The kid had nothing. Daddy. Bird. Having prevailed in a battle with a toddler, Ben continued their quest through the warren of added-on corridors.

Ben pointed to a guest room door and told Ivan. "This is where you were made."

Ivan looked at Ben like he was being silly and began vocalising 'Daddy bird' in a dozen different tones.

Ben slowed down in front of a supply cupboard while a rickety older couple walked by. Once they had made their way past, Ben opened the door and took what he came for. Verification: a bar of soap.

That night after dinner, Janelle went to the sink and closed her eyes at Ben's request. He washed her hands with the soap. She couldn't see its cornmeal colour or read the carved logo, but her sense of smell was legendary, at least in their house. He towel dried each finger.

Ivan watched, not sure what was going on, but practically bursting with anticipation anyway.

Ben told her to open her eyes and he covered the soap with the towel.

They used to play this game more often, one making the other close their eyes and name the flavour of some food, or identify a fragrance. It was always something lovely, a precursor to a gift or a kiss. His mother had watched them do it a few times early on and made some comment about their gorgeous marriage. But Janelle would always win and Ben never would. Eventually that became part of too large a pattern between them, so Ben stopped instigating. His mother noticed the absence of the game too and had probably deduced they were headed for divorce. Janelle probably thought they were headed for the poorhouse. Ben wondered if Ivan had an opinion. There were sides to a family like there were sides to an argument and all of them were wrong. Alek's model, however cracked it was, agreed with him: in this version, the marriage would work out.

He let go of her hands. "Sniff," he said.

She held them to her nose.

"Clove, a woody smell; sweet but musky. I know I know it."

Ben waited for the light of recognition. He gave her a clue – raised eyebrows and a glance at Ivan.

"Got it." She brightened, grabbed for the soap and turned it over to see the name of the hotel. One kiss on the cheek for Ben. "Thank you. It's a very romantic thought."

"There's more where that came from," he told her, about to tell her everything.

"I should hope so. It would be ridiculous for them to mail it out one little bar at a time. Let's clean up."

"No." He had to keep her from housekeeping. "I picked it up myself. I went there."

"All that way? When?"

"Daddy bird!"

"This morning. Wait a second. I think you'll be surprised."

Ben pushed a chair out of the way so he could get to the window.

"Our life is about to change," he said.

"What does that even mean?"

"Daddy bird!"

"Enough sweetie," she said. "Did you teach him that?"

"Daddy teached."

He had teached it, but he didn't slow down, and clicked open the safety bars on the window.

"Stop it. I don't want Ivan seeing how to do that."

Ben felt evangelical, like Alek must have felt about the nappy. He wanted to share everything with Janelle. He wanted to take her up over the city and show her the sights from above. The window open, he stuck his face into a warm breeze. It would provide perfect lift.

Janelle panicked at his eagerness. She became frantic, grabbing hold of his ankles as he climbed out onto their tiny balcony. "Please! Ben!"

"Let go."

"I won't! Come back in here! You can't leave Ivan and me like this!"

"What on earth are you talking about?"

His bewilderment stopped her and she relaxed her grip for an instant. As soon as she did, he leaped onto the ledge. Janelle gasped.

"Daddy bird!"

And he was airborne.

Ruth

Ruth tightened the tourniquet on the old guy's arm and tapped his vein three times with her forefinger. Holding the needle in her other hand, she went in. Even though he was sawdust dry, the sharp knew where to go. She scored the thin, dark line and pushed the vial onto the end of the barrel to collect.

He flinched. She tightened her grip on his elbow and said, "Won't be long. You're doing great."

Outside, it was already getting light. She could send this over to pathology, check on the patient next door, write up the last notes, give handover to morning staff, dive into rush hour and be home in bed by 7.30 a.m. Golden.

"Is that enough, you little vampire?"

Ruth looked down at the vial in her hand. It was full, out of suction. She'd taken more than she needed.

"Yes, that'll do."

"For you, I can spare it," he said with an unappetising leer.

Ruth straightened herself while stabilising his elbow,

so she could slip away without jeopardising the vein. She shaped her mouth into a smile as she unhitched the tourniquet and pulled the needle out.

Pressing the wad of cotton to his arm, "Hold this there. Firm," she said.

Nurse! Please come here! I'm dying! Come right away!

The old man was sitting still, his two fingers obediently placed against the cotton at the joint of his arthritic arm. He was staring idly at her chest, not alarmed in the least.

Ruth took two steps towards the corridor to see if anyone was answering the call. The cleaner wheeled a bucket past, in no particular hurry.

Anybody! Please come!

No response. The voice was coming from the next room, where ancient Bella was slowly being taken down by pneumonia. She hadn't eaten in three days. It couldn't be her. Even if you were right in front of her lips her voice wouldn't have been audible over the rattle of her lungs.

Please!

"Aren't you going to straighten up?"

Ruth looked behind her. Using his chin, the old man gestured at the needles and their wrappers on his tray table.

Ruth came back in with her efficiency face, lips tight. She collected the vials to send out, sweeping up the rest and dumping it into the yellow hazards container on the wall.

A quick squirt to disinfect her hands and she entered Bella's room. No one else was there, aside from the wheezing patient. Ruth peered closely. The old woman's eyes were shut, as they'd been for most of the last two nights. Her breaths were paced as far apart as could possibly sustain an old woman's circulation. Each inhalation was the system's last fail-safe. An old machine breaking down. She wouldn't have been able to call out, let alone be heard in the next room. Ruth rested her hands on the bedrail. Bella's fingers twitched, as if trying to reach them.

You heard me! Thank you so much. Please, don't do anything. Just stay.

Her lips hadn't moved.

Ruth imagined that she had imagined it. That was the answer. Bella's breathing stopped and started again.

"I'll be here for you," Ruth said.

A reply came: *That's all you need to do. Sit.*

Ruth dragged the visitor's chair close to the bed and sat.

Surely this was the result of working too many nights in a row. The diurnal pattern of normal humans had been desecrated. Her brain told her to sit down because she needed to sit down.

Bella's staccato continued. Ruth massaged Bella's cool hands in the warmth of her own.

Ah, lovely, that's what I want.

Ruth nearly let go of her fingers when she heard this, but managed to maintain her composure. She was having a paranormal experience, right there in Room Nine. A container of lavender lotion sat on the side table. She poured some into her hands and smoothed it up and down each of Bella's fingers.

Ahh.

Ruth couldn't contain herself. "May I ask: what is it like?"

Pleasant enough, considering my regrets. She paused. *My girls.*

"I've met your girls. They've been here every day looking after you."

I know. They've been trying, but they're never going to have peace. They haven't given any to their mother. How can they find it without her?

"There isn't always harmony in families," she said.

I'm talking about my family. My girls have provided me with more than my fair share of grief. Unspeakable times. It doesn't matter now, naturally. It wasn't on purpose. Even I can forgive the past. It's strange. All these pieces you hold so tight, they drop their weight as if they never mattered.

This had to be projection. Ruth's notion of death had always been a slow balloon trip upwards, letting go of ballast all the way. This was Ruth telling herself how she always thought it would be.

"What do you see?"

Words don't do it justice, but it's familiar. Deja vu, I suppose. It's the same place I was before I was born, I think. How do you like that? All these decades of worrying and it's the same place you started. Why don't we spend more time being scared of birth?

Ruth had never had that thought before.

The breathing grinded down, impossibly slow. Ruth put two fingers on the underside of Bella's wrist and sensed her pulse coming to a halt. She controlled the urge to call a code. In three minutes the room could be filled with medics and equipment, shocking and cracking Bella back to life. But Ruth was confident the boxes had all been ticked. The family knew this was coming. They had been there every evening until visiting hours were over, waiting for her to finish fading. Nothing needed to be done except to let her go.

Ruth said, "Don't worry, I'm here until the next shift comes on. Till your family comes in, whenever."

You're a dear, but I doubt I'll be that long.

Ruth had to file that comment away too, because as soon as she heard it she realised that the breathing had ceased entirely. Bella had stopped. She died with a half-smirk on her face at 6.54 a.m.

A doctor was called to certify. Afterwards, Ruth closed the door to the room and hung up the laminated sign to keep staff or family from walking in until they spoke with the nurse in charge. She made the call to notify one of Bella's daughters but was only able to leave a message for her to phone the ward. A terrible message to leave on an answering machine. Ruth told the relevant staff that Bella had been tranquil when she died in bed. The family was welcome to contact her if they wanted to hear it from her directly.

Trying to race through all the paperwork and formalities

before morning traffic started in earnest would be futile. Ruth noticed Charmaine passing by. She was on the morning shift; she might help with washing the body.

"I suppose so," Charmaine said. "She was on my corridor. Bella was such a sweetie."

"Perfect. I'll meet you in her room in five," Ruth said, returning to her notes.

It's too early for dead people.

Ruth, who was not feeling at all tolerant, called after her, "Then go work for a dermatologist."

"What?" Charmaine said. *I'm going to lose half an hour on this, and then God knows how much longer holding a box of tissues for the family whenever they show up—*

Ruth stared at Charmaine's face. She was smiling. Not speaking.

And I'll probably still be given a full load of patients for the shift.

It was her voice, clear and hollow, like it was coming from under a sink.

Ruth said, "I'm sorry. I'm all over the place this morning. I'll see you there in five. Is that all right?"

"I said it's no drama."

Ruth watched her walk away. She could hear, she realised, other competing voices rushing together as all the nurses passed by, starting their shift.

Above it, she heard Charmaine, *How about I'll be there in ten and she can get a head start on the wash?*

Ruth had evidently endured some sort of accident in her brain or spiritual awakening, she wasn't certain. Home and bed. That was all she had to achieve this morning. Home and bed.

The cleaner pushed his broom by the station and glanced at her with a nod. "Morning, Ruth." *Poor thing. Looks like she's been chewed up, spat out and given to the dog.*

He gave a sympathetic grin and moved further down the hall.

Over at the corner desk, she heard the nurses and their grumbling array of concerns.

Tubes tied… the linen cupboard's a war zone… Not awake at all… I hate working with that useless cow… suctioning trachy snot all day… shower the old geezer… smooth satin pants, party pink… I could sleep for another six hours…

They didn't know sleepy.

As Ruth moved closer, the steady trickle of their thoughts grew into a rush that she didn't want to hear. Charmaine, leaning across the counter, waved her away, "Don't worry. I'll be right there." *If she had a regular man she wouldn't be in such high gear all the time.*

Ruth waved back at her, "Charmaine, forget it. I've got Bella." She swung by the supply room, picked up a metal basin, washers, and two large plastic bags, and turned back towards Bella's room. This was a job she could do without the extra commentary.

When they were young, Natalie could sometimes read Ruth's mind. It was an older sister's prerogative, she'd said. The first time it happened, they were coming back from the library and Ruth had been daydreaming. Natalie held out her arm to keep her from walking into traffic. What Ruth had been thinking about was leaving home. The grander plan was to complete her hospital training and go overseas – anywhere she could use her skills. Morocco looked exotic enough to fit her fantasy. Once she learned the language, she would find her way into an expatriate existence in an apartment in a busy corner of some ancient city. Near a market. From there, she would travel with her notepad and not much more, finding home wherever she went. Occasionally, there would be a lover who would bring her hashish and poetry. In exchange, she would make him tea and he would be allowed to sip from her worldliness. She was all of fourteen and had shared these thoughts with nobody.

As they crossed, Natalie said, "Not that I could ever stop you, but do you need to go so far away?"

The trick, Natalie said, was a kind of maths, achieved through a consideration of Ruth's expression and everything else going on. No hocus-pocus, she said, just thinking. She collated the facts. It was situational telepathy and it meant Ruth's private thoughts were often discussed before she even had the chance to act on them. Ruth could never return the favour, no matter how many clues she had. Natalie generously shared her own secrets though, to keep the relationship balanced. So unlike other kids her age, Ruth had to get by without the romance of her own loneliness. It was comforting and intimidating, especially from an older sibling. Like having a twin who was always one step ahead. Still, it wasn't the same as picking up every stray thought in a hospital. Ruth had entered another realm.

She pulled the washer between each of Bella's toes. You clean the feet last, once the body is adjusted to a respectable position, before it all gets too firm. Bella's face looked reasonable. No matter how weary and waxy people looked at the end, Ruth often detected a gleam of relief, as if they had been wandering down the wrong path for decades and had finally arrived at the place they had been searching for. The place they had been before they were born.

Bella's silence put Ruth at ease. The prospect of finishing this task and going back to the uncensored voices of the corridor did not. There had to be a reason. The first manifestation of a tumour. A sleep-deprivation psychosis. A nurse's uncontrolled explosion of empathy. Each scenario suggested a hospital admission was in her future.

Bella's smirk lingered. It suited her. At the wink of death, if you were free enough and another person was nearby, you could grant them a second way of hearing, so that you could be heard. If the circumstances were right, as they had been with Ruth, the sense could expand and the recipient would hear others too. That must be it.

A low gurgle escaped from Bella's yellowy lips in confirmation, but her expression remained the same.

Who knew? It was as sound an explanation as any.

On the way out of the car park, the attendant gave Ruth the usual, sarcastically chipper "Good morning!" The joke being that neither of them wanted to be where they were.

It was followed by *Lord, take me if I'm working here at her age.*

Driving home, unjustly ensnared in the rush of people going to work, Ruth tried to consider options. The thought of calling in sick didn't appeal, largely because she didn't feel sick. But the prospect of returning that evening to a storm of comments darting past her every minute – that would unwind her, fast. The whole raw mess of the hospital's consciousness, staff and patients seething with all their indignities – that would be unbearable.

Four nights on in a row never yielded her best brain. She was tired and there was one more night to go. This was all a dream, her mind urging her body to draw the blackout curtains and tuck herself into bed. She would try warm milk first and if that didn't work in half an hour, she would go straight for the pills. By the time the half-hearted winter sun set that afternoon, she would be awake again and all would be quiet. The thoughts in her head would be her own. It sounded like bargaining. In the same way she knew she wasn't sick, she knew the voices would still be there when she woke up.

Possibly, this was the beginning of what would become of her. It was undeniable that she had reached 'her age'. The hours and shifts had sculpted her into the same shape of the old nurses who had taught her. She would run to them with questions and respect, thinking to herself, *Lord, take me if I'm working here at her age*. Had any of them heard?

If the stock market kept working for her, she could quit in five or six years and stay home with her feet up. Other than that and until then, it wasn't a buffet of options.

As she pulled into her parking place, she saw Martin getting ready to drive off.

"Morning."

He rolled down his window. "Hey."

He was cute, younger. Forty-four, as if such an age implied youth. He was the only one there who was at all neighbourly. They shared a balcony and sometimes she watched him out there from her living room when he did sit-ups in boxers and not much else. She'd entertained some entertaining thoughts, but nothing within the kingdom of likely. Martin had fixed her sink when it clogged. Ruth had bandaged his elbow when he fell off his bicycle. It was like that. His presence one wall away provided an acceptable minimum of companionship. What did he get from her presence? She braced herself to find out.

"Just coming home? Lucky you, all done for the day." *Getting to spend the next few hours lounging – lucky. Wait—* "You worked last night?"

"Yes."

"There was noise in your kitchen, around eleven. I thought it was you. I definitely heard noises."

"What was it?"

"Music, and dishes-in-the-sink sounds. Your nephew?"

"Alek hasn't been around here for a long time. And he made a big show of leaving the keys when he left. Could it be the new people on the other side?"

"No, definitely your kitchen. Should I go up with you?" *Please please please don't say yes. I'm so late already.*

Ruth couldn't help smiling, which must have made Martin wonder.

"Thanks. I'll be fine. No burglar would have bothered staying through the night. It must have come from your other wall."

"Yeah, maybe." *I hope she doesn't get killed.* "You'll call if you need me?" he said.

Ruth promised, and Martin sped off, leaving her to wonder how she would keep a straight face with anyone.

For as long as she could remember she had never completely believed what she said to people or what they said to her. Conversation seemed inherently dishonest – a mixture of showing off and begging, in one form or another. Now she had a different way in. The first thing she would do would be to call up Ben and see what he really thought of his dear old mother – assuming the burglars had left.

It would be ironic but make perfect sense that since she'd managed to move one tiny notch upmarket, thieves would have finally decided that she was worth their trouble. Her place, on the second floor and far from the stairs, wouldn't have been their smartest choice. Still, she unlocked the door with minimal clicking, pushing it open like you would on a crime show.

It was a deco two-bedroom, with too many bookshelves holding too much stuff. Because of the usual disorder, detecting a break-in with certainty might be difficult. The cordless phone had been left on a shelf, not in its cradle. This could have been her doing. A stack of magazines for recycling had been tipped over. This could have been spontaneous. Or not. Ruth took a step back. No sounds. There were alcoves and corners where someone could easily hide. Still, she felt confident as she ventured in, ears alert. If anyone were there, she would hear them think.

She called in through the doorway, "Hello?"

She expected an internal *Oh shit!* No sound.

She stayed out in the open so she could, in theory, run back into the hall.

No sound.

Ruth picked up the phone to carry from room to room,

in case she'd suddenly need it to call for help or beat someone over the head. That's when she saw it, next to the change bowl on the dining table – the open container of chocolate milk. Alek's calling card.

"Alek?"

She walked through her five rooms looking for more signs.

When he'd left two years ago, he told her, "I need to find my way out of this," but wouldn't say if he meant this apartment, this city or this life. His departure was not up for discussion, but afterwards Ruth used her off days to scour the city for him. The staff at the restaurants where he had worked didn't know and didn't care. He was replace-able. The ones that were advertising for kitchen help didn't remember taking any applications from "an extremely en-ergetic, handsome young man, a little under six-feet and pale, with brown curly hair and," she would add in a lower volume, "a sort of preoccupied expression on his face."

She hoped to see his backpack in the middle of the spare bedroom. Its lumpy, sometimes smelly presence would mean he had parked himself here again, if only for a few nights. It would be an excuse to call Natalie.

No backpack. Silence.

He would have been out there, coping well, until again, inevitably, he couldn't. Then he'd come back to whomever would have him. This was his habit. Ruth could relate.

No backpack, no shoes, no pile of laundry.

The whole pattern was worse if it was your son. Alek had talked rings around psychologists. He had denied the need for the meds, he had taken them to please his parents, he had pretended to take them to please himself. And every once in a while he would vanish for weeks and months, returning healthy, smiling and in a new pair of jeans. Maddeningly, he would maintain that he had never been far away. It wore everyone down. In the end, Natalie ran out of wisdom and Peter resorted to tough love. Alek wasn't interested in that scenario.

That was when Ruth had stepped in, her goal being to play good cop long enough to get him back home. She offered him the spare bedroom of her new apartment and the independence he was always talking about. Living closer to the city would help him connect with more like-minded souls.

"Connect to druggies," Natalie had said.

He behaved though, living with Ruth for nine months, not always making sense, but not disappearing as much. It was his longest stretch anywhere since he'd left school. It was on and off for another two years after that, with him utterly abusing the freedom. Ruth said she meant to do right by him, that she didn't want to see Alek discarded to the wind. Natalie told Ruth that she was undermining their parenting.

"Where is he right now?" Natalie asked, during one of their last civil morning calls.

Ruth, home from work five minutes and without a clue, said, "Out."

"Discarding himself to the wind, I imagine, and using you and your spare room when it suits."

"But I've made it plain that life here has limits."

"Have you shown him? If you don't show him, then somebody else surely will."

"I told him—"

"Deeds, not words."

Natalie and Ruth stopped talking about Alek and things became cordial between them. A few months after that, as if he was the only thing they had in common, Natalie stopped calling altogether. To make it all worse, this was when Alek announced he was leaving. He tossed the keys on the dining room table and told Ruth, "Won't need keys anymore where I'm going."

Ruth called Natalie that night and cried that she had lost him too.

Natalie said, "Of course you did," and hung up.

Ruth called back, but Natalie hung up again.

Ruth gave it a day, then several days, but Natalie didn't pick up. At first she thought it was a wound that could be healed with time and a few of the right words. But Natalie never responded. When Ruth realised that her sister had truly cast her adrift, it was a disaster. The first year after the divorce had been a similar disaster, but it came with the consolation that natural and sensible laws had prevailed. All

Ruth knew was that she had tried to be good and her sister had cut her off. Even after a dozen pleading, apologetic letters, Natalie granted her no more contact. It was as if Ruth had sent him away.

No, he didn't need keys. Alek had come in through the balcony. He had smashed the smallest pane to unlatch the window and climb in. The broken glass had been brushed into a neat pile with a blue Post-it marked "Sorry" on top of it.

When he first moved in, she imagined him losing the keys on a regular basis and they discussed hiding a spare set.

"There's nowhere you could hide them that a thief who looks for keys couldn't find them," he told her. The balcony, he added, was far too vulnerable.

There was more promising evidence of him in the kitchen. On the window ledge, a beef bourguignon was steaming in her blue baking dish. The aroma didn't feel right for the early hour, but she knew she would be grateful for it later. He'd used or spattered every utensil, pan, cutting board and counter, leaving it all where it had landed. The deal had always been that she would do the clean up. Did he really break in to cook?

The blank dining room wall she had just walked past grabbed her attention. Ruth took two fearful steps backwards. Her favourite painting was gone. Over the undusty rectangle where it belonged, another 'Sorry' Post-it.

Over many years, Ruth had struggled to internalise the patient drone of every yoga instructor and therapist she had ever seen. Their soothing mantras filled her head at times like this. Breathe out. Drop shoulders. Let the heart get sadder. Let it expand again. Let it adapt to change. Let it adapt to loss.

The picture was Ruth's sole remnant of the solid first year of her marriage. A small framed sketch, a busy bright stick figure of a city skyline floating in a golden patch of wilderness. She'd managed to hold onto it through all that had happened since – a grab bag of homes, a grab bag of men, and the kids slipping off into their lives. It was one of the few belongings that she had counted on to keep her company in old age.

Ruth sat down at the table and stared at the space on the wall. When she'd first seen the sketch, she had liked but not loved it. It was a very lesser Paul Klee though, and somehow within their reach. If they skipped a few treats for a while it could be theirs. That first year they were going to build an empire. They would make investments, in art, of all things. Not loving the picture provided her with confidence that she would be able to part with it when the time came to cash in. She had shared all of this with Alek one night and asked him if it had been hubris?

"Does every action have a pathology behind it?" he asked.

He was right. That was when she detached it from her marriage and from its potential value and came to like the picture for what it was.

Alek had never stolen before, not that she knew of. He hadn't needed money, just an occasional bed. Paying jobs materialised for him like they would for no one else – Ben, to name one person. Alek would excitedly play along with the formality of work for the first few pay slips and then get bored. There would be a disappearance, a bewildering excuse, and another promising job. This was why Peter had lost it. They couldn't control him if he was financially viable.

The break-in indicated bad things. His flightiness had finally led to trouble. He was in debt to someone – someone nasty? The sketched city in its frame was bouncing in his khaki army pack on its way to a pawnshop or art dealer. It was about to be traded for a fraction of its worth. Every possibility was a sinkhole.

9.30 a.m. and still not in bed. It was officially too late to even try. Her body's clock had fully turned over into the next day and there was so much else to think about that sleep was becoming unlikely.

Every once in a while, Ruth felt the necessary pull of destiny. When she'd eloped, when she finally took the kids and left, when she'd switched to night duty, when she'd bought this apartment. In each case, she couldn't have done otherwise. Her decisions had been inevitable. And now, she

decided, her sudden talent of deep listening was meant for
Alek. For years, she had wanted to get closer to him, to her
own kids, to everyone, always closer, by asking questions.
Always closer towards a vanishing point of data that might
help her understand why they did what they did. That's
why the gift had arrived. She would hear what he thought,
find the painting, know what kind of help Alek needed and
bring him in from his fog. This too was fated. There was no
need to call the police. There was no need to call Martin.
And nothing to tell Natalie yet.

All she had to do was find him. She taped a piece of
cardboard over the broken pane to keep out the wind,
changed out of her work clothes and, with no idea where
she was going, set out.

The air was colder than the winter light had her believe.
Three long streets to the park. He would be sitting on the
bench near the lake, his arms extended, holding the picture up towards the thankless sky. It would turn out not
to be about money. It would be some sacrifice to beauty.
He would say, "It needed a drop of sunshine." If she found
him, Ruth was sure she could lure him home. At first sight
she would listen to what was brewing behind his words. It
would save him, save the whole family.

But Alek wasn't on any of the benches that she could see

and she was already beginning to ache from the chill. With bleary energy, she trudged out of the park and towards a street corner where there was a pawnshop. Maybe that was his destination.

The times he stayed with her had been calm, mostly. When their schedules overlapped, he would cook, blowing out any savings on the best cut of meat or bottle of red he could find. On his own nights, he kept to his chocolate milk and baked beans. He would demurely fan his farts into the room. This, in the middle of pep talks. He was always advising her, about scuffles at work, about men, about the sorry turns her life had taken and how every one of them had been necessary so she could become the mind-blowing individual she was. It was nice to have that on tap.

The few times when she had tentatively suggested that he stick with one job or hold on to his money, his face went harsh. Or, heaven help her if she asked him what was on his mind. He hated that, but most men did.

Once, she noticed that he was staying home from work with a cold.

"Do you want me to give them a call so they can find someone else tonight?" she asked.

"Don't mother smother," he said.

Natalie hadn't laid eyes on him in almost three years at that point, so the warning was understood.

That sharp edge would soften just as quickly, and he'd go back to spinning out tales of things that he couldn't have done, trips he couldn't have taken to impossible places, even stories about her. Natalie found this talk too chaotic, while Ruth believed that listening openly to whatever he had to say was exactly the medicine he needed. When she felt nursing concerns creeping in, every word out of his mouth indicated another symptom. Preferring the notion that her nephew was merely special, she chose to ignore that line of thinking. If she allowed him to spin out his stories long enough, he would reach a rational core. In the meantime, he kept her enthralled and that was enough. She listened to him the way Alice Liddell would have listened to *Alice in Wonderland* – dazzled to find that she was inhabiting someone else's fairytale.

Leaving the park, she passed two Pilates-postured young mothers, setting out on a cardio walk, ploughing the street with their children strapped into superior strollers. They trotted along in silence, with a cloud of extra dialogue around them. Out of the static, Ruth heard, *This is getting very old.*

Ruth was able to tell which of the two had had the thought, but she wanted clarification: was it motherhood itself or simply the walking partner that was getting to her? What would she rather be doing? Mopping down the sick and the dying all night? Searching pointlessly for a wandering nephew with your stolen artwork? Ruth would settle for a dull walk in the park with an infant.

After all the kids she had swaddled, when the time came to push her own in their inferior strollers, there was no room for pleasure. Even when they were asleep she was transfixed by what they would need when they woke up. Alek and Sasha, though, they were a joy to handle. It was the one thing she could do for Natalie. Getting them to settle made Ruth feel invincible.

The afternoon that Alek left he allowed her one desperate hug. Ruth topped it off with, "You still feel like you did as a newborn, on the day we first met." It was indulgent, but she meant it as a last-minute bid for him to stay. "If you stay, I won't judge."

"That's why I'm out of here," he said.

The pawnshop wasn't going to open for half an hour. There was a cafe with a direct view where she could warm up while she waited. When its door, stuck with winter wetness, opened, she fell into the middle of the room. A dozen patrons twitched in her direction before returning to their friends and newspapers and coffees.

I've got three tickets and we're going!... They can wait for their water... I'm hanging out five more minutes and then leaving without a note...

Trying not to hear any casual disdain floating in the air, Ruth scanned past the counter to the kitchen. Cooking had been the thing that nearly kept Alek on a straight path. He'd said it was mindful, constant and productive, and would always be his fall back. She looked for his face behind the counter, but didn't see it.

She set herself up at a small table next to the window like a regular woman of leisure. Her eyelids felt papery from being open so long. Each blink made a click. Still, he might pass by.

The words around her drifted in.

Friendly or not-so-friendly… The thing to remember is that she doesn't mean it… I really don't need a second coffee…

If there were a cure for this, it would have to be sleep. When the waiter approached, his mind a race of table statuses, Ruth asked for a large latte, as if that was a good idea. For her main course, a raspberry and white chocolate muffin with a few mitigating grains and seeds. Alek would walk by the window, see her sitting there, come in, make fun of her order and all would be right.

They don't care if I pay with change…

Don't listen. Don't distinguish the words. Think of a clear field of colour, a favourite shade of orange, an enveloping afternoon sun – the orange disc floating above the manic town in the painting inside of Alek's backpack. He must still be close. Or was he on a bus already to parts unknown? No. He would come back to her, with the painting or without it, but in his heart, he must want the connection. There was no managing her thoughts anymore.

Don't scratch, leave it alone. The cream will fix it…

And this wasn't the place to empty her mind.

Whenever he returned from one of his blank patches with unlikely details, she tried to accept his words as having their own kind of truth. She didn't fully believe what he reported, but maybe he had drawn himself into another dimension for a week or a month. How else would he have returned from his internal neverland in one piece? She once put this forward to Natalie, who tightened a smile and said, "Maybe you'd like to try some antipsychotics too?"

Ruth suddenly saw herself, sitting alone in a cafe window, trying to chase away voices.

She cancelled her order and left, taking the straightest route home.

Pressing the door open without a sound in case he had returned, she saw that nothing in the apartment had changed, except that the piece of cardboard on the balcony window had blown off, chilling the room. Ruth added enough tape so that the window was good and ugly. Another broken thing to be dealt with at some unspecified later date. A pill, a shower, and she fell into bed. Closing her eyes to another field of colour, she tried to focus on something plain, the shade she'd painted the apartment. Helping her choose, Alek told her that each of her selections was obvious and demeaned her individuality. She went ahead with antique white. She launched herself into its safety.

Dah-dah, dah dah de dah-da. Her new phone had arrived already set to an *I Dream of Jeannie* ring tone. That also needed to be dealt with. She woke up fast, still drugged and stumbling to find the phone. It was on the table, next to the chocolate milk.

"Alek?"

"No, it's me. I'm at the bookshop. You're still home?" *When she's on nights it's like going out with a zombie.*

So: sleep wasn't the cure.

Ruth had been seeing Simon on and off for four months, but they were still mostly on good behaviour. Several times she had explained why she preferred to work nights. Obviously, it hadn't sunk in. At least this would be an enlightening phone call.

"I'm sorry. I had to take a pill and then I forgot to set the alarm. It was a long shift. I just woke up—"

That's just perfect. I was all ready for the Italian. Too much to ask for a bit of attention, a lasagne, a decent bottle. "So did I hear right? Alek's back?" *She was too attached to him when he was gone and now he's back. Perfect.*

"In a way. He came to the apartment, but left before I came home. He made me a beautiful beef bourguignon, if you can come by for a quick dinner—?"

"We had plans." *Her place would only bum me out tonight.*

He had been so tender the other day. "I know it's a bit

late but with a little time I could come meet you."

Doesn't sound like she's dying to.

Increasingly, she wasn't.

"What do you want to do?" he asked.

"I don't have hours and hours at this point, I'm sorry."

"I understand, you didn't do it on purpose," he said. *Screw this.*

He was understandably over it.

"Look," she said, "is it too late for you to salvage the evening with anybody else?"

"Yeah, no. I'll be fine." *I could have gone to a movie. I could have gone to the gym. I could have done a trillion other things I like to do but now I'm outside and hungry and it's all shot.*

"What can I do to make it up?" Her eagerness to please was as unappetising as his sulking.

"Don't worry about it." *How about being awake when everyone else is? How about using some salt when you cook. How about not jumping up and running off to the bathroom when we're done screwing?*

"Simon?"

"Yeah?" *To top it all, I hear feelings coming.*

"I'm truly sorry about tonight. I think my work schedule may be crushing into each of us a bit. I have a contract so I'm going to be on nights for at least three more months. Does that put you off?"

"No." *Why don't you call me in three months?*

"How about this? Let's put it all on pause for three months, so this doesn't happen again, and see if we're more in tune later on? That sounds like a solution, doesn't it?"

Wait? She's dumping me? She stands me up and now she's dumping me?

Ruth said, "It would be easier for both of us. If it's right at all, it will still be right in three months. Don't you think?"

I don't believe this. I'm getting dumped, on the phone, in some bookshop, when I did not make one wrong move whatsoever.

Ruth wanted to open her heart, wanted to let self-awareness and patience flood in. What she said was, "That's right. You did not make one wrong move whatsoever."

His grammar had always pissed her off.

Driving to work, Ruth was still riding the rush of the phone call. After months of perfectly amicable time together, with a few promising conversations, even a couple of bouts of better-than-adequate sex (when she didn't always rush off to the bathroom, thank you very much), she had finally been able to listen to the real him. Gaining access to the full hostility men stored up had usually taken her much longer. Getting off the ride before she felt sick was an even greater accomplishment.

How much investment and effort had hanging up on

him saved? Half of the workshops she'd ever taken had promised such self-actualisation. This talent could bring her closer to now.

The prospect of ten hours at work with her amplified sense of hearing increased her buzz. She wouldn't waste her shift by paper chasing at the nurses' station. She would sneak away from the gaggle and linger in the rooms with the patients who were awake. If they thought she was fat or skinny, or whatever they saw from their angle on the bed, was of no importance. They were sick and what they cared about was themselves. The chronic, living in their parallel universe. The atheists, struggling to locate some logic in their illness. And the young ones, finding out that sooner or later everybody goes to the hospital. She wanted to listen to their synapses and cells, so she would know how to help.

All the patients she had nursed over the years who had lost speech, all the times she had wished she could comprehend. With a job on a neuro ward or in a nursing home, she could be nurse of the year, pulling sense from all the mangled mouths and minds. They would tell her where it hurt and when they were hungry. She would see that they received what they needed. And all their desperate visitors with their secrets. She'd become the expert on servicing all of them, the patients, their families. She'd be run off her feet, but she would be their medium. She'd get her own TV show. Her foot rested heavily on the accelerator for most of the drive to work.

As promising as the evening ahead looked, she was even more eager for the next morning. She had left the front and back doors of her apartment unlocked. After the shift, Alek would be sprawled on the sofa with a container of chocolate milk. She would listen to him, follow the maze of his brain, wherever it led. He would feel better for it, loved. She would bring him back to Natalie, like a maternity nurse with a newborn, and they could start from scratch.

As she pulled into the lot, the surgeons and scrubs and cleaners were all on their way home. This she hated, the absence of the warmth of a simple evening. It was a trade she had to make after the marriage, when the extra pay couldn't be ignored. Before and after work, she would sit with the kids for dinner and breakfast so they could pretend to be a family, and that was enough. Natalie had been her mainstay in those years. No telepathy, but at least enough contact to keep Ruth from flying apart. By the time the kids found their way out, Ruth's body had adapted to the reversal of nights. The fact remained that she enjoyed the ward at its quietest hours. No doctors, no procedures, and no visitors. The patients were usually as stable as they were going to be. If they weren't, she was there for them. Nights were the purest form of the art.

Ruth found a parking spot near the central stairwell. She draped her uniform over her wrist, gripped her swipe card in one hand and a big bag of low-fat mixed-grain chips in the other.

Ruth girded herself for handover. The patient lounge had been painted breast cancer pink, which only accentuated the lifeless pallor and internal grumblings of the night staff.

When she's in charge, nothing gets done... I hope I get the cute guy in seven... If I get all of mine to sleep by nine, I can sneak out to call about the car...

She didn't want to know any of it. Her mission was to bring her full attention to the nurse in charge. With effort, she focused.

As the status of each patient was recounted, the stray thoughts became softer, like she'd turned a dimmer switch. With more concentration, subterranean voices reduced to a hum. Sweet peace! This was the protective filter she needed. It meant she could listen to one person at a time.

Allocation gave her the far end of the corridor. Most of the patients down there were stable and would sleep for the next few hours. Come two to four in the morning though – the witching hour – any one of them would be as honest, as vulnerable and as angry as a patient could be. She would be their confessor and servant.

Once she had eyeballed all her beds, hearing nothing but weary snores and the occasional trill of a monitor, Ruth gathered her files and headed for a desk at the south station. At least she would get notes done and keep a safe distance from the caramel corn someone was making in the kitchen.

No buzzers rang. No one fell. No one woke up. She felt almost cheated.

At five-thirty in the morning the linoleum silence was broken by a ding. The lift doors parted, right across from Ruth. A suited, silver-haired man stepped out, looking both ways.

This is four, isn't it? "Pardon me miss, is this east?"

"Yes, it is, but visiting hours don't begin until eight."

He looked at his watch. "This is close enough for me. I'm after my son. His name is Vince Moriarty. A skinny kid," he said. He held up his index finger to jog Ruth's memory. *Too skinny. Like this.*

Vince Moriarty, who was seventy-two, had been in for a week, waiting for a bed in Oncology.

"I'm certain he's sleeping. Can you come back in a few hours?"

Who cares if he's sleeping? "I only want to sit with him till he wakes up. I took two buses just so I could be here before the workday starts up."

"I shouldn't let you—"

Ah, yes, but you will. He went past her as if he hadn't heard, looking for a sign that would show room numbers.

He was the father; this wasn't worth the argument. She directed him to Vince's room, following at a respectful distance.

"Thank you. I'm Con. I'll be so well behaved it will knock your socks off." *Nice lady. Not bad.*

That would have been the perfect time to press the mental mute button, but she had been waiting all night to see what she could do.

Con didn't falter or pause, as most parents do when they see their child in a hospital bed. Instead, he marched over and inspected his son's sleeping form like it was merchandise.

Not looking too strong today, buddy boy.

Ruth lingered at the doorway.

With the same scraggly index finger that he'd held up as evidence of Vince's shape, he poked his son in the chest.

Vince stopped snoring and opened his eyes. "Pop?" *Unbelievable.*

Con hovered his face over his son's and grinned. "Aren't you pleased?"

Vince focused, then laughed in Con's face. "Who made you finally make the twenty minute trip?"

"Nobody made me."

I doubt it. Vince laughed again. "And who let you in?"

Con smiled, gestured back towards Ruth. "This law-breaking nurse over here had me come see you. Specific instructions to wake you up. She wanted me to use a scalpel, but I said I didn't have the heart." Con performed more for Ruth than for Vince. "It's been our busiest week, one of the new stores wasn't happy with a shipment – wrong colours. Some idiot doubled their order in aqua.

Every day was a shell game. You're lucky to be laying low."

Con took the visitor's chair right next to the bed. Vince smiled at his father. *How do I tell the big man I'm dying?*

His family didn't know yet.

Con gleefully nattered on while Ruth listened to Vince. *Pop's been one perfect bastard for his whole life but that doesn't mean he deserves to watch everyone else go first.*

Con went on. "What are the odds of us getting some Scotch in here? While we're at it, how about a cigar?" He turned to Ruth. "Mr Health Nut, the one in the hospital bed, quit years ago, but I didn't. I'm no quitter – and look at me. Still fighting fit and ninety-four. And a half."

Con finally noticed he was the only one talking. *Why's everybody so quiet?* "So what's the plan here? Don't you need your bed for somebody sicker?"

"Pop. I need the rest. They're building me up." *For chemo.* Vince looked at her. *Please, let's tell him the truth and get it over with.*

"No fooling? Like a truck. I can see that. They're whittling you away to more of a pencil than you already are." He looked around, shaky. *Somebody, talk to me. What's the girl here for, decoration?*

Vince said, "It's the hospital food, I swear. As soon as I'm home—" *Once the stairs become too hard, I can sleep in the living room.*

Ruth finally had to step in. "How about if I try to arrange a meeting with the doctor for later on today?"

"What for?" Con asked.

"To discuss Vince's current situation," she said. Her gravity would get them past all of their posturing.

Con put his dry knuckles against his dry lips. "His situation?" *They said it looked like an infection.* "Vince, what situation?" His tone shifted from friendly to not.

What did she do? Vince struggled to get back to where they had been, "They're trying to find the right antibiotics, Pop, that's all. I'll be better—"

Con turned on his son with rage, "That's not what she meant, Vince. Tell me what she means. Cancer?" He looked at both of them. *Tell me what's goddamned real here!*

Vince was watching his sand slip away. "Yeah. Same as Uncle Nick."

"Bad?"

Vince covered his eyes. "A few months, a year maybe." *There.*

"And how's that next few months, year maybe, going to go?" He turned on Ruth. "My brother-in-law, we had a year of suffering. My wife, two years. So what have you experts done – cut the dying time? That's progress?"

She kept his gaze while she listened.

Con shook his head, *Should never have bothered coming. He's already dead.*

This was a hard one, but it would lead to a better understanding. "A sit-down with the doctors can be very useful. One thing I can tell you without doubt is that the kind of suffering your wife or your brother may have gone through isn't necessary anymore."

"It was three years ago and it was in this same lousy hospital," Con said. *It's over. My boy is over.*

Ruth was out of platitudes.

Con glared at her. *Foolish girl.* In another second, he would say it aloud and she wanted to speak before he did.

"I'm sorry," she told Con. To Vince, "I can leave word to see about having some sort of family meeting this morning to bring everyone together. How does that sound?"

Con snorted. "You'll forgive me if I take a pass on your family meeting. Not my scene. Bye-bye." Without looking back, he headed out to the corridor and the lifts.

Vince blinked at her. *And who exactly is going to come to this family meeting? Pop was it.*

Ruth told Vince, "He needs time."

Vince held his head in his hands. *Time.* "You're the night nurse. You shouldn't have even let him in." *Should have kept your mouth shut. What were you thinking?*

Vince had wanted his father to know. Con had asked for the truth. This was certain. Con would have been the perfect advocate for Vince. It's what a parent has to do, whether they want to or not.

"I can have the social worker come to a meeting. They can talk about services we can put in place and counselling that might be appropriate," she offered weakly.

Services. Vince didn't look up.

"Is there anything I can do for you?" she asked, leaving out the usual 'else'. She prayed that there was.

He shook his head, looking at the empty visitor's chair

Reserve me a quiet room at the other end of the hall.

Driving home she replayed the scene over and over, putting herself in all the roles. Her single error had been letting Con onto the floor. After that, she had been responsive to the information she was given. But it had gone so badly. If the words she had been picking up weren't some underground stream of truth, what were they?

The inner monologue had to be where truth resided. It was jabbering, but it was more authentic than what people said out loud. For Ruth, when her stray, unvoiced feelings bred hope in a hopeless situation, or when they drove a hole straight through something solid, she accepted that thought as her new reality. For the past twenty-four hours she'd been given access to this vein of honesty in others and she had accepted it as fact.

But it wasn't. It was only more role-play – for an audience of one. Even the thoughts she was now having on the entire subject were suspect. As far from the truth as anything else.

These problems circled her so furiously that she was barely aware of having arrived home. From her parking place, she saw the light on in her kitchen and the top of Alek's head. His hair had grown out in a jumpy mop that was bouncing across the room. Was she ready to hear what was going on underneath it?

She walked up the stairs slowly, almost dreading. She stopped outside her door with her key poised near the lock, so nobody would walk by and find her snooping in the hall.

What was on his mind?

Aniseed, anus, annual, manual, mammal.

He was associating, which he sometimes did out loud. Harmless.

Don't stay past breakfast. Remember: only visiting. Don't stay long enough to cause trouble.

She could accept that too, as long as he was safe and well. Only visiting, can't stay long. That was practically his motto.

Ruth took a step back from the door and turned his thoughts down. This wasn't the answer. If she heard more, she would give it too much weight, as she had done all day. Misinterpretation was inevitable. The family already had enough of that.

All she could do was restrict her thoughts to things that had happened. What did she know? Alek had broken in, taken the picture, and made the beef bourguignon. He came back, and he was zooming around the kitchen making something else. Whatever thoughts he kept to himself wouldn't tell her much more about the world.

They would have a nice conversation over a warm meal. Words were not deeds, but they were another way people communicated. She would listen to his words and watch his eyes when he spoke. She promised herself she wouldn't listen beyond what he said out loud.

Ruth walked over to Martin's door, rapping softly until he opened up. He was dressed and smelled like deodorant. He was drinking a banana-coloured milkshake. "Breakfast."

With her shh finger in front of her lips, she led him inside to his kitchen.

"Alek's next door."

"I know. The music was on until two and started up again at six."

"I'm so sorry."

"No, I—I had a friend over. A good night, actually. The beginning hint of a possibility. I think. Alek was good enough to play DJ," *Thank God Ruth wasn't home with one of those silent evenings of hers. She would have heard it all.*

Ruth didn't know where to put that one.

"What do you want me to do?" Martin asked. "I can go over there with you if you're nervous."

"No. I want to watch him first, from here," she said, pointing to his balcony.

"Help yourself," he said, swigging down the last bit of milkshake.

She pushed the glass door open, crouched down, and padded out into the chilly morning air. The kitchen view was blocked by a bag of groceries on the counter. When she scooted to the far end of the balcony, she was able to see Alek.

It was like a glimpse of a rare bird. He had pulled down the alien-shaped juicer she hadn't used in years and was working through a big bag of oranges, juicing them into a jug. Calm and confident in everything he did. She could have been watching Natalie.

From the corner of the balcony she saw the Klee hanging in its place on the wall. Whatever time it had seen with Alek was over and it was home.

The drabness of the rest of the room disturbed her. A coffee cup she'd left on a shelf. Stacks of framed pictures she hadn't hung. She'd been there all these years and hadn't moved in. Boxes of books she hadn't read and wasn't going to. Simon was right. It was depressing. The place looked like she'd never believed she was going to stay. Even the bland colour of the walls.

Martin whispered from the doorway, "I'm heading off. You sure you're okay about him?"

"Yes."

"Then you let yourself out. It'll lock after you."

"Thanks," Ruth said, "and congrats on your possibility."

"We'll see."

Martin smiled as he left. Ruth wondered what she would have overheard the night before. No, leave it alone.

With a sick feeling she wondered if she had been too

harsh with Simon. Why should someone have to think grammatically?

She looked at her apartment again and it made her sad. For her next contract, she would switch to days. That would force the question: what to do about all those silent evenings of hers?

Dah-dah, dah dah de dah-da. Ruth dropped to the ground in case Alek could hear. The phone in her bag eluded her hand and she didn't manage to silence it until she had crawled back inside Martin's kitchen.

It was the hospital; Bella's daughter wanted to speak to her. Could they transfer?

The daughter blessed Ruth. She thanked her for all the good care she gave to the sick, for all her good work, for being with her mother at the end. Then she got around to the purpose of the call. "Please tell me, did she say anything?"

For an instant, Ruth had all the power. She could have told more, could have mentioned forgiveness and could have mentioned the return to the place before birth.

She decided to answer the question. "No, I'm sorry. You saw how quiet she was those last few days. It meant she was comfortable. It was a peaceful morning for her and that's all we could have hoped for."

The conversation made the daughter break down anyway.

"We didn't always understand each other," she confessed.

She listened to her sobs. Ruth's eyes went glassy. The woman apologised for taking up important time with her crying. Ruth was trying to assure her that it wasn't anything to be sorry about when the woman hung up, leaving Ruth holding a dead phone.

After absorbing the silence, Ruth decided to take action. She fiddled with the keypad until she had switched to the Brandenburg ring tone. There, that was one job done. Another would be to call Simon later.

A peek outside – Alek was busy at her fridge. He knew her schedule. He was waiting for her.

It was still early. Natalie would be at home, getting herself ready for school. The phone didn't have Natalie's number programmed in so Ruth had to work from memory to make the call. Not to tell her anything in particular, just to try.

"Hello?"

"Nat, it's Ruth. Please stay on."

Natalie stayed on.

Ruth didn't try to listen. A simple sound, an acknowledgement would do. Steam rose from her breath three times. She lowered herself to the floor. "Nat? Are you there?"

"Yes. I'm here. I'm thinking. Give me a second."

Good. Thinking was good. Ruth slid herself across the tiles till her back rested against the refrigerator. Take your time, she thought, stretching her legs. Choose your words, don't choose your words. It doesn't matter. Ruth could wait all morning to hear what they were going to say.

Sasha

T minus five. Sasha ducked through the party to tell the queen of the cater waiters to kill the lights.

A super thin Goth, she was primping six lilies that leered out from an umbrella stand. To answer him, she kept a hand on one stem for support. "No can do. Fire regulations."

"Seriously? This entire place is a death trap. It would be for five minutes. Till she gets here."

"Can't."

"Pretty and please," Sasha batted his eyes.

The chicklet batted hers back.

Sasha's phone vibrated near his crotch.

"At least point me to the switch?"

She exhaled, turned, and glanced at the far wall. "Five minutes is all you get," she said.

"You're a legend."

"We've never met." She returned to the lilies.

Sasha opened his phone. It was Giordana. He dodged into the bathroom corridor to muffle the crowd.

"Where are you?" he asked, picturing her lost on a bus

somewhere or, worse, still back at his apartment, jetlagged.

"I'm outside of a place called The Lion and The Witch."

"Brilliant."

"But it looks like an antique shop."

"It is. Giordy, trust me. Come inside. Look for the dusty-looking guy wandering around the furniture."

"Okay, yes… I see him through the window."

"Good. Then point yourself at the painted blue wardrobe near the back of the shop."

"All right."

"Tell Dusty you want to look inside it. He will ask you your name and you will tell him your name. He'll check a piece of paper on his desk and believe me your name is on it."

"Okay."

"He'll unlock the door to the wardrobe and let you in. Go in. There's a spiral staircase and it's a bit dark. Be careful on the way down. I'll be there waiting for you."

"Ace."

"Ace yourself. See you in three," and he folded her off.

Sasha pushed his way towards the light switch, plucking a glass of white from a passing tray. With respect for neither aroma nor integration of flavours, he sculled it and took a quick stock of the room. The low rumble of conversation. The tink of other people's wine glasses. The faint air from a cigarette that someone was daring to smoke. Everything was stellar.

No sign of Damon anywhere in the room. Would it have been such an inconvenience to show up?

Sasha cleared his throat.

"Everybody! She's upstairs. Be quiet!" he said, and turned off the lights.

Cave silence. He was proud of himself for assembling such an obedient crowd on three weeks' notice. Nothing to do but wait for Giordana to get up the nerve to ask to see inside the wardrobe.

Connor was in arm's reach, near enough so that sandalwood was in the air. They hadn't seen each other in two months, easily. This was how it was getting with his friends, no matter how close. Sasha came up from behind, slipped his hands into Connor's front pockets and pulled him back into a grind. Connor complied, falling against his chest.

"You don't bring me flowers," Sasha whispered into his neck.

Connor crooned back, "You don't sing me love songs."

"It's inspirational really," Sasha said, "When you think of Barbra's fortitude, not getting her nose done, especially in that half of the seventies. The pressure from Hollywood must have been hideous."

Connor agreed. "Is Damon coming?"

"He was invited, but—" Sasha detached.

"I'm sorry."

"His loss," Sasha said, moving on.

Light at the top of the stairs. He could hear Giordana thanking the proprietor. She started down.

"Sasha?"

This party would be good for her. A warm welcome back. Her colleagues, at least the ones Sasha had been able to track down, were wetting themselves already. Best of all, no family. Aside from him, of course.

He took two steps back to keep his fingers on the switch in case a fire did break out – which would have sucked.

Giordana was halfway down. "Sasha?"

Switch on.

"Surprise!"

The money shot: Giordana sputtered superbly. She didn't turn thirty-five for another two months but that's what added to the stupefaction. Her friends yelped and surrounded her at the bottom of the stairs. It was done. They fell all over themselves, raving about the venue. *The wardrobe!* They had probably all done their theses on the Narnia books and were busy looking for Jesus in the umbrella stand.

Giordana made her way through the crowd, with sheepish hellos to Sasha's friends. They were on message. They said all the enthusiastic things you say to someone's cousin you've met about twice.

Finally, the trays started to fly out of the kitchen. The chef had made a lot of noise about his innovative spring rolls – chicken and sprouts, smoked salmon and horseradish cream, and so on. If that's what was passing for cutting edge. As long as he kept to budget and everyone was smiling. The whole evening was a gentle kickback from the manager. It was intended for Sasha's employer, but Sasha was fine about accepting it for himself. After all, he was the one who found the restaurant in the first place and had organised half of his agency's functions down there when it first opened. He was their word-of-mouth.

Jonah, one of the dishiest clients Sasha's group had taken on in recent months, was pacing in solitary circles on the outskirts of the room. He looked like he was pondering the paint job. Slinky otter build, an author. A thoughtful type, when he wasn't fretting about his sales. Sasha had invited him as an offering to the birthday girl. Jonah would fit snugly into Giordana's milieu. He hooked Jonah's elbow, trajecting him back into the thick of the party. "My friend, you're up-current from the servers and the ladies. Not remotely strategic." Jonah smiled and accepted, as he did most of Sasha's suggestions.

Giordana stumbled the gauntlet, amassing a shelf-load of book-shaped presents, three bouquets, and two bottles of champagne (from Sasha's friends), each wrapped with bows. It had been a while. She'd stayed with him for the two nights before her flight a year and a half earlier. It was always two nights on either side of a trip. If he hadn't happened to live near an international airport, he wouldn't see her at all.

Truth was, she probably took him about as seriously as a reality show. They were different genres. Deep and narrow, meet broad and shallow. Alek was really her preferred cousin, with all of his drama and trauma. Even if he was tripping his balls off somewhere, he was the one she worried about. Whatever, the point of this party was fun. Sasha would score points with his parents and Ruth for having made the effort.

Giordana arrived in front of him and opened her arms, nearly dropping all the gifts. "Sasha. This is above and beyond."

"You are," he said.

Giordana threw her arms around Sasha. That realness of her breath and body slowed him down. When she'd left for Hiroshima, it was the same hug. It hit him in two parts. The first was the surprise that such a serious person would show such tenderness. The second was a question: where was this feeling in him? Her hugs always made him feel defective.

"Thank you so much for this. I normally let my birthday slide."

"That's why you needed it."

Jonah tried to veer away from the love huddle, but Sasha kept one arm around Giordana's waist while the other reeled him in. They were free, single and straight. Why not?

"Giordana, this is my favourite author, Jonah. Jonah, this is my favourite cousin and professor, Giordana."

"Hi Jonah," Giordana said with a minor expenditure of air. New people didn't wow her. It was as if they still had to prove themselves relevant before she would pay any attention.

Fortunately, Jonah had come prepared. "I Googled you this morning. Your research is terrific. The rebuilt cities thing is – I know you're working in an academic realm, entirely fact-based, but it has a poetry—"

"Thanks."

Maybe it was from teaching for so many years, but she could telegraph both gracious and dismissive with one innocuous word. Like Damon. The incapacity to fake friendliness. Still, Jonah's effort should earn him at least a soupçon of warmth.

Sasha dug a thumb into her side and grabbed Jonah by an elbow to make them squirm closer. He leaned towards Giordana's ear and said, "Jonah is an extra decent guy. Be civil a minute. You two will fall in absolute love."

He pictured their wedding.

A static charge between them all – her woollen skirt? – and they slipped from Sasha's grip. The oxygen in the room seemed to suck in and suck out.

Facing her intended, Giordana began to make friendly. "So, Jonah, what's your book about?"

Sasha knew Jonah's pitch – he had written it – so he unhooked himself from their conversation and left to go solve the mystery of the non-existent drink in his hand.

He appraised the scene again. His regular crew had dissolved into its usual arrangements.

No Damon in sight. There wouldn't be.

The blondest, slimmest server conveniently appeared. Retrieving another glass of wine, Sasha flirted. The guy lingered, his body curving in Sasha's direction. They discussed the creative challenges involved in devising a genuinely new spring roll. The server appeared to be willing. More than that, he proved to be dextrous, tapping his number into Sasha's phone with one hand while balancing a tray with another. It boded well.

Sasha entered his number under the name "Party." He could be erased or given a proper name later, as needed.

Giordana's friends, who were clearly away from their home turf, were floundering, peering around like they were lost, diddling their wine stems and nervously eating all the spring rolls. Sasha moved in closer so he could assist. They gushed with appreciation for the entire evening. Cindy, their ringleader and a bit of a Valkyrie, did most of the thanking.

After the conversation died back, there was a moment's dead air. They were all used to such things, he was sure, but that was Sasha's cue to talk. "Do you think she'll ever run out of ruined cities?"

"I didn't mind visiting her in Warsaw, but I don't think so. It's sad," Cindy said.

"Sad for the cities or sad for her friends?" Sasha asked.

"Both, really," she snorted, surprising herself, and looking to the others, in apparent amazement that a common publicist possessed such rare and refined wit.

He liked them; he could access them. One day they could all spread out a blanket and play Scrabble. Her crowd would surely play for blood, but he imagined he could awe them with some of his words. They could have a picnic in the park. Sasha would insist on doing the catering himself.

One of Cindy's backups asked Sasha, "So who's Giordana talking to?"

He turned to see that she and Jonah had moved their conversation to a corner sofa. It had gone far beyond enforced good manners. They were sitting close, nodding at each other as if it didn't matter what they were saying. Their necks were turned towards each other in goosy symmetry, like salt and pepper shakers. Three fingers of Jonah's hand were perilously close to Giordana's thigh, lightly tapping the slim wedge of sofa between them. As if they were waiting for what's next.

"An author," Sasha said, absorbing the view. His silly plan had worked. On his cousin's behalf, he was scandalised.

Cindy assured the sidekick, "She must know him from a conference or something like that."

"Ten minutes ago she didn't."

Cindy raised a glass of sparkling water, "Then give yourself a toast."

For the next hour, Sasha massaged the room. He supervised the flow of provisions, he circulated in and out of conversations. The mission, as ever, was to prevent hunger, thirst or boredom.

A few more introductions were made – some business, some pleasure – but none gelled as solidly as Giordana and Jonah, who hadn't budged from their spot, except to scoot closer to each other. They were visibly smitten. Jonah's fingers were now, indisputably, skimming against her leg, and Giordana's arm was propped against the sofa, the inside of her wrist supporting his neck. If she chose to scratch her cheek with that hand, they would be forced into a kiss. Sasha was turned on by the success of his match.

While Giordana hadn't often launched into theoretical discussions about the destruction of cities with Sasha, she had often and freely confided about her romantic mishaps. He suspected that she did this for two reasons, both lame. One: Sasha, even at this advanced age, had never told his parents about his personal life. Though they would have to be wearing leather blindfolds not to notice, they officially didn't know. All this meant was that he was unlikely to repeat anything about anyone else's life back to the family. Two: Giordana – adorably – believed that Sasha's carnival of fuck-buddies had yielded something remotely shaped like insight.

For a few years, her details had actually been interesting to listen to. At one of the universities that was perpetually courting her, an almost divorced and allegedly genius professor on the hiring committee was consistently making all the right noises. Downside was that he still lived with his wife, so the most that judgemental Giordana ever allowed were overtures. At the exact same time, she was having a run of resolutions and relapses with a city planner with whom she claimed to have zero in common. He lived in Mostar, another decimated city. She had to exploit a few fellowships to keep that one going. This all made for many trips to the airport and many frantic what-should-I-do nights in Sasha's kitchen. In the space of one miserable month though, both contestants, for their own unknown reasons, retreated. After that, utter dryness. As far as Sasha knew, only her research grants and her friends accompanied her on the long dip into the unpartnered middle-of-age. Not that his own prospects were so flash, but never mind.

Sasha approached Giordana and Jonah on the sofa, to see what they could be talking about for so long. She didn't even turn in his direction. Jonah did, and gave a look that you're never supposed to give your publicist. Sasha backed away, more than content. If this thing stuck, Sasha would get all kinds of family cred.

Giordana's crew kept a similar distance from her for the remainder of the night while Sasha, his mission more than completed, relaxed and gravitated towards his friends.

Connor had managed to drag Tim along. Together forever, they weren't moving in their usual tandem. They were
clearly having an off night. Sasha first met them during that
brief slice of time when he and Damon were pretending
to be a couple. They all double-dated. Connor and Tim's
extreme seniority as a pair made them mentors. They dis-
pensed advice often. They were kind, they were good hosts,
they'd survived a decade plus. That was enough to make
them an institution. Afterwards, they kept Sasha.

"Neither of you two were up to the task," Tim told him.

"Damon pulls the pin me and I cop the blame?"

"Yep," Tim said. "You'll slow down one day. Maybe
when you hit your forties. Or when they hit you."

It was irritating when Tim got superior, especially when
Sasha was sitting at their table and eating their risotto.

Tonight, Tim and Connor stood close but silent. Their
gazes and goatees drifted away from each other. Connor
looked tense. Tim, the same, plus pouts.

His observation of Tim and Connor's body language
was interrupted by the sight of Giordana and Jonah
heading for the spiral staircase. This was staggering. Her
departure was as much of a gift as her arrival. Giordana's
cluster of friends, their mouths hanging open, looked
extra bereft as she circled up the steps. Jonah followed
close behind.

"So, has the party gone according to your wishes?"
Connor asked Sasha.

"More or less."

Giordana had ditched her own birthday. Amazing, awesome even. Sasha felt that he owed her friends goody bags as compensation. His attention returned to Connor and Tim. "You two all right tonight?"

Connor shrugged. A few feet away, Tim gave a yawn and gazed philosophically at the doors to the kitchen.

"We shouldn't have come out," Connor said. "It's just a bad patch."

"My cousin would tell you that she appreciated your effort, but she's already left."

Sasha fantasised that he could do for them what he had done for Giordana and Jonah. He tried to remember the trigger. Disgruntled as Tim and Connor were, they allowed Sasha to gather the two of them into his reach. He touched them at their wrists, making a chain, skin to skin to skin.

"You're being creepy," Tim said.

Sasha's silent benediction provided them with a life of harmony. He felt another charge.

Connor jerked away.

Tim's posture softened.

"Everything okay?" Sasha asked. Neither of them looked in his direction.

Tim's hand rose up and gave Connor a sincere and tender Vulcan salute. Back in the day, the two of them were Dungeons & Dragons freaks, so one could only guess at the geek shorthand they – thankfully – kept to themselves.

Connor offered a Vulcan hello in return, with every bit as much poignancy.

"Get a room," Sasha said and pulled back.

They didn't notice. They sank towards each other and into a greeting so full of forgiveness that for an instant Sasha thought he might cry.

As the other guests found their reasons to leave, Sasha was desperate to try his hand once more. He was unnerved, but also buzzed by his powers of persuasion. It had to represent an evolution of his skill as a publicist. His fingers regularly typed releases that could entice an audience. Why couldn't they matchmake?

The vampiric chicklet who had pointed him towards the lights was standing over a side table, pouring the dregs of a dozen wine glasses into a plastic jug. He circled around her, faux-casual. He would set her up with anyone at the party, whomever she wanted. Kind of like a bonus.

"Was it a good night?" he asked.

"A friendly enough crowd."

A spring roll splashed from a glass into the jug and they watched it unravel. Slices of vegetables floated in chardonnay and merlot effluent. "Human beings are revolting," she added.

"Agreed. But I was wondering if I could introduce

you to any of the ones here. Anyone not so revolting?"

Her lips went up in the shape of mild distaste. He felt like a pervert on a bus.

She said, "Look. Thanks. My boyfriend's waiting back at home. He drives a van. He's not so chilled about me roaming. Get the picture, honey?" She raised the jug at Sasha as a toast and a sign to get lost.

He wanted more subjects to practise on, but everyone was already going home.

Giordana and Jonah were on the bench under the kitchen window. They jumped up guiltily when Sasha came in.

Giordana said, "You're back." A line rarely delivered with enthusiasm.

"Yes, I'm back," Sasha said, only mildly put out that he felt so unwelcome. They were, after all, his doing.

Standing there by the cupboards – as if they'd been, what? Getting ready to make a torte? – Giordana took Jonah's hand in hers as a statement.

"I had a lovely birthday. Thank you."

A less obvious but just as beatific thank you smile appeared on Jonah's face.

Giordana swung Jonah's hand lightly. Sasha had never seen her this demonstrative.

He knew next to nothing about Jonah, he realised, except

that he was young and had survived The Wrong One. That was his description of his adulterous ex-wife, and the title of his book. A total puzzle how he squeezed a publishing deal out of it, or why straight people cared so excessively about a little side action, but the concluding paragraphs – which were all that Sasha had read closely – implied that he would not fall for the wrong one again. So that was a hopeful morsel.

"Everybody's welcome," Sasha said.

A more considerate host would have decamped to a nearby hotel room for the night so the couple could rattle the plaster in peace. Sasha didn't have those manners or that kind of money. And he wasn't about to sleep on his own sofa.

"Good night," he said instead, excusing himself to his bedroom. He would put on the white noise machine.

Giordana stopped him on his way. "Were you going to have a shower?"

"I wasn't planning to."

"That's terrific," she said, tightening her clasp on Jonah and leading him towards the bathroom. With no self-consciousness at all she pulled him in there and closed the door.

"I'll need my toothbrush though," Sasha called out. Instantly, a hand opened the door and delivered it with – so thoughtful – the tube of toothpaste. The door shut just as quickly.

Sasha stood there, looking at his toothbrush and eaves-dropping.

"We don't have to do a thing," Giordana said.

"I know. We don't."

"We have all the time in the world, so slowly, slowly."

"Slowly, slowly," Jonah said.

The rustling of clothes. A long silence. Were they examining suspicious moles? Jonah chuckled, as if he had lost balance taking off his jeans. Sasha listened as Giordana helped him recover with some kind words. The worshipful quiet continued until one of them turned on the shower.

Sasha sank down outside the door and balanced the toothbrush across one knee and the toothpaste on the other. He rubbed his face with his hands, like he was trying to wake himself up. There was conversation about aeroplanes, something else they evidently shared, followed by some questions from Jonah. The pauses in between their talk grew till it was only the shush of the shower. They went at it, with no regard for water conservation. It was their first time, so there would probably be no giggling – a random assortment of tricks that had worked on others before and might work tonight, all with the goal of making a good impression. But everyone wasn't like that.

Damon said that the first hours of a relationship were the most exciting, that particle of time before you knew too much. The romance could still be exactly like your fantasy. A truly observant person, or someone who hadn't been waiting for love since he was ten, would not have been so quick to sign a twelve month lease with the issuer of such a statement. Sasha had not been this astute. All he saw was poetry. Not to mention the sex.

That was then. To a certain degree, it still was. They had been apart longer than the minuscule seven months they had been together. Pitiful, but it was the biggest heartbreak he could point to. Damon had called up last week, like he had in the past. He'd been clear – again, like he had in the past – and said that he didn't want to stir up anything, that he was merely after an evening of company. Sasha's ego was at its lowest ebb, so he walked the ten blocks to Damon's new apartment for not quite break-up sex, not quite make-up sex, but sex. They played house for a few hours after that, made dinner, read on the sofa with their legs intertwined. It happened once a month or so. Then Damon would show him the door. Like he had every time before, Sasha came home, downed a glass of triple-strength chocolate milk – a special-category prize for not asking for more – and went to sleep. The next day he'd left a message inviting Damon to Giordana's party. No reply.

An unseemly grunt emanated from the bathroom. Was Sasha really going to wait around to hear Giordana hit her high notes? Before heading for bed, he brushed his teeth at the kitchen sink.

"It was totally bizarre," she said. "One second I was making my way down the stairs and wishing I could hug every person in the room – and disappear at the same time, you know me – and then you introduced Jonah and suddenly his was the one face I cared about."

"Do you feel the same way about him today?"

"To be truthful, more so. I have to send a note to Cindy to explain. What I did was just wrong."

Giordana shoved her cereal bowl to the side and opened her laptop.

Sasha considered his father's rule about reading material at the table. The thought sidetracked into his father's likely disenchantment with other aspects of Sasha's daily life. "They all saw how involved you two were with your conversation. I'm sure she'd understand," Sasha said.

"Still, they travelled all that way and I behaved like an adolescent."

"Did you feel like one?" Sasha asked. No answer. Giordana was pecking out her apology. "Do you think you'll see Jonah again while you're here?"

She didn't look up. "There's a mean deadline he has this afternoon, but he invited me over later. We'll see what happens. I might stay over there. He lives alone."

Was he supposed to feel bad that he hadn't vacated last night? "Sorry about the pull-out sofa."

Giordana chewed on a nail and spaced away into email land while Sasha observed her for crucial indicators.

An occasional fond, fluttery upward gaze – check.

The feeling that Sasha and his questions and the screen in front of her were all an interruption from the one thing that mattered – check.

"Can you tell me what you're feeling?" he asked, trying to understand his power.

Giordana looked over the edge of her computer at him, annoyed, but willing. It was his kitchen, after all. "Strangely calm," she said. "But it's been a while for me. Maybe that's what it feels like at my age."

"Stop downplaying it. What what feels like?"

"This," she said, waving her hands in the air. "The tickle. The wondering what's going to happen."

"Does it enter into your calculations that he happens to live here?"

"Details, details. I'm not having calculations," she laughed, getting back to her screen. "The truth is I don't remember feeling this positively about anyone. Severe fondness. He seems real."

Offhand, like that: real.

Giordana looked at her laptop. "Message here from Alek."

Sasha couldn't even remember the last time they'd spoken. His brother's name felt like something that had been attached to his ankle when he was a child.

Giordana read on. "It's a weird one."

"Aren't they all? Where is he?"

"Java."

"For the coffee?"

"He's been there a while. I managed to track him down for a phone call once or twice. I was going to try and get there to see him, but he discouraged it. He said family still confuses him. Full of plans though, living quietly." Giordana scanned his message. "Working on rice paddies in season. When it gets cooler he takes tourists around the sights. He swears the language is easy to master, so he's in demand for whatever he feels like doing on any given day. He can quit a job every week and still find work."

"Sounds ideal."

"He says that he's suffused with earthly treats."

"Starting with way too much kind bud."

Giordana said, "What?"

Sasha didn't bother.

"He says he's lonely for love and hopes I'm not," she read.

"There: you have something to report."

He envied Alek, wearing out his welcome across the continents. But leaving the rice paddies wouldn't cure the loneliness. You could be in the middle of the most crowded dance floor in the most crowded city and you could still be in solitary.

Giordana started typing. "I'll tell him about the party. Did you ever bring him to the Lion and the Witch?"

"He hasn't come through this way in a while."

"You have to take him there. Opening the doors to the wardrobe, pushing the coats back, and that staircase down. The brilliance of it. That's the universe he wants to see." She looked up meaningfully to force eye contact. "He would adore it." Sasha didn't care enough about his brother. That was the family's reading.

Before Alek left for good, that last time, Sasha had received a surprise mid-afternoon visitation. He was with a client when Alek appeared at the cubicle, standing in the doorway and singing, "What the world needs now, is lunch sweet lunch." The client was bewitched, which made it forgivable. If the client hadn't been, the scene would have had less appeal.

The occasion was a request for money, to get him to Hong Kong. He was going to vanish again.

"Does Ruth know?"

"No. She'd try and stop me."

"Like she could."

"True. But you won't."

Sasha felt accused. "So you're pulling a geographical?"

"If you're asking if I think everything will be better where I'm going, yes. I'm sure of it. All I need is my pack and my ticket. And that's where you enter the picture."

Sasha gave him the money, partly because he trusted that Alek would be able to sustain himself, at least for a while. He'd squirrel out a decent existence for ten minutes or so, get himself laid a bit, charm a few strangers. Then he'd wander off, and eventually come scurrying back.

Sasha also knew their parents would benefit from Alek's absence. A bit of time would be a healthy thing for all concerned.

Giordana typed with vigour. "I'm going to suggest that he try to find his way home, if he can. How are your parents with him these days?"

"Calm and relaxed, as long as he's in another country. I don't think he'll come. He'd be scared they'd net him," Sasha said.

"Net him?"

"Stick him in the bin. Let a shrink take over. One of my father's clunkier threats."

Giordana shuddered. "Don't let my mother hear that. She has another year till she's one herself, God help us all. And she's still rabid on the subject of Alek. She has a thousand theories about his brain, not that anyone's asking. At any rate, he doesn't seem to need a bin in Java."

"He never did. He's merely a touch too whimsical. He'll survive," Sasha said.

She tilted the computer screen towards her so she could give Sasha a professorial glare.

"Do you really think that's enough for a person? Is that all you're attempting to achieve every day, survival? We need more than that – we all need friends, intimacy."

"Suddenly we all need intimacy," he smirked. Giordana said nothing.

Alek only made contact when he wanted something.

After all these years and all her smarts, Giordana hadn't worked that out. Alek's real reason was somewhere in that email. Sasha didn't feel like discussing it further.

Giordana worked through her disapproval of Sasha's brothering by writing back to Alek, big time. In exchange for his one-paragraph greeting, she sent back five screens of news, detailing her research, the party, and telling him all about Jonah, as if he'd really care. Let the record show that at no time during her ongoing, director's-cut commentary about the composition of this masterpiece email was there any talk of paying for his ticket home. All she was giving him was a letter. She wouldn't hear from him for another six months.

While she typed and rambled, Sasha called Connor for further confirmation of what seemed to have happened the night before. Connor's report: "Honestly, Tim and I have been at each other a lot for minor infractions lately. He didn't want to go last night. But right in the middle of it all, we had this mutual *moment*. It was what I've always imagined electroshock therapy must be like, except not as sedating. What it was was thrilling." Connor's voice hushed here, in reverence, "Like sudden perspective. We remembered how we felt. You were right next to us. I have no idea why you should be part of the moment at all because you're so coarse when you're in party mode."

Never mind all the flattery and gratitude, Sasha felt heady with the fact that he was the one responsible.

Giordana had stopped typing and stared dopily off into space.

Sasha's pride in what he'd apparently achieved flipped into fear that he didn't know why it happened or how long it would last. What if it worked like Ecstasy, and a day of pleasure was paid for by three days of overwhelming, dark funk? He didn't want to be responsible for heartbreak. If her newly found fondness was his responsibility, he felt duty-bound to let her know. The goal wasn't to piss on her parade, per se. Tim and Connor could handle this love wave as well as any turbulent wake, but Giordana was delicate. He didn't want her jumping blind into this situation that might go wrong. If she accepted that it was a hex of some sort, she could develop the appropriate wariness as protection. The only way to convince an academic, though, would be with empirical proof. Which meant he would have to do it again.

They were heading for the cafe when Sasha phoned the office to say he wouldn't be coming in at all. Giordana, who had never worked a normal job in her life, seemed to get a contact thrill from his call. If he could wow an academic with a slack workday, imagine what his next stunt would do.

The usual assortment of freelancers were spread out with their computers and coffees, forcing Sasha and Giordana into the threadbare loveseat next to the counter. Fortunately this provided the clearest view of the main stage of the place, the espresso machine.

"This has been my new regular for the past month," Sasha said. "The coffee is sublime."

Giordana doubted. "My coffee house in Hiroshima had women in lab coats. We'll see."

As they sat down, Giordana examined the wallpaper. It was pink stripes of cats in dresses putting on prissy tea parties, alternating with brown stripes of dogs with moustaches drinking coffee at some Roman train station. "Is this all cryptically sexist or am I hypersensitive?"

No response required.

Sasha knew the people who worked here, their names at least, and he thought one or two of them would, if he orchestrated it well, accept a furtive touch. Especially if there were results. It would make the point to Giordana and spread a little happy at the same time.

They ordered from Vanessa, a nose- and lip-ringed blonde in her twenties with a purple G-string that rode higher than her jeans. She had been a chemical engineer but was fed up with the culture and had taken a personal style vacation so she could find "one goddamned guy on my wavelength." Vanessa passed their order to Nick, working the coffee apparatus. He was a slight, angular dude with a buzzcut and concave chest who – when Sasha had initially come onto him – revealed, A) that he cared deeply, to the point of documentarian obsession, about single source beans, and B) that he was woefully straight. Together, Nick and Vanessa were visually pleasing. They were money sexy – those who would pay to watch sex would pay to watch Nick and Vanessa have it. Presumably the two of them had considered it before, but if he bestowed his special blessing, they could revisit the possibility. And Giordana would be there to witness.

While Sasha waited to strike, Giordana pumped him for Jonah data. He gave his book report on *The Wrong One* and what he had gleaned from interviews. It actually provided enough personal info to serve as a romantic CV. Giordana grinned or blushed with each detail. The more she did the more Sasha toned down his talk. He had never seen her this neurosis-free about anybody. The bottomless cheer coming from She Who Always Knew Better was beginning to skeeve.

When Vanessa came back with Giordana's double espresso and his latte, Sasha set up the play. He asked her, "So how much longer do you think you'll stick around here?"

Vanessa leaned in for a confidential reply. "Another month or so, max. The work doesn't worry me, but my mortgage does."

Sasha said, "And your manhunt?"

"Nada," she said, drawing a line with a finger across her neck. Vanessa addressed Giordana as she poked

Sasha's cheek. "Unfortunately all of the good ones are—" and she turned towards the kitchen without finishing the sentence.

Sasha called his next target. "Hey Nick?"

"Hey Sasha?"

Sasha raised his latte in Nick's direction.

Nick whipped his kitchen towel in thanks.

Sasha turned to Giordana, "Don't you think Vanessa and Nick would make a sweet couple."

"Are they?"

"No," Sasha said. "Not yet."

Far from being the type to pay to watch, Giordana was not even likely to obtain jollies by speculating about the personal life of others. "So you actually have no idea if they're suited," she said.

"But wouldn't they look good together?" He didn't truly know if he would be spreading love or disaster.

Vanessa went into the kitchen, passing Nick. Neither regarded the other with the slightest of glances.

Giordana exhaled, indicating the drying up of her interest. "Yes, it would be a veritable banquet for the eyes," she said, gazing longingly out the window for intelligent conversation.

"Right," Sasha said. "Why not?"

Vanessa emerged from the kitchen with an eggs Benedict and a salad. She delivered it and returned, stopping next to Nick to rinse out a tray of dirties for the dishwasher.

"Watch this," Sasha told Giordana, and he walked over to the bar.

He leaned across the polished counter top till he was in arm's reach of his two intended, and beckoned them closer. The only reason they complied was because Sasha was an absurd tipper.

He had never touched them before but he gripped them each on the shoulder, with a possibly forgivable zeal. His thumbs brushed their necks. "You two do a fantastic job," he said.

As he reached the third syllable of 'fantastic', he closed his eyes to dial up a grand partnership of equals. The jolt came right on time and the bridge circuit released.

Yes. They were sharing a sudden secret.

Sasha moved away to let nature or whatever it was take charge. "Really, keep up the good work," he said. He was, by now, irrelevant.

Vanessa twisted her body towards Nick's, maximising visibility of her G-string, and told him, "I need to head back to the kitchen."

"That's cool. I'm here. Whenever." He thumped his hand on his chest twice.

And before she pushed through the swinging door, she lunged out to give him a peck on the cheek. Vanessa looked startled as she disappeared into the kitchen. Nick went after her.

They were besotted. And unlike the other couples, Sasha

barely knew them. This was more than lucky matchmaking. He would hook up every damaged person he could find. The glum ones looking down, the stupidly hopeful ones watching the sky, all of them. The solitary freaks. They would each get what they wanted.

Sasha returned to the table, hands out, "Did you feast on all of that?"

"Yes, your hunch proved correct."

Sasha sat down. He was trying to be as rational as he could about something this ludicrous. "No. That wasn't a hunch. I did it."

"What?"

"Yes. Didn't you see their expressions when I touched them? How they changed? I'm a conduit. Look at you and Jonah last night."

Giordana's smile froze into a line of patient impatience. "That's giving yourself quite a lot of credit."

"How else can you explain the sudden coupling? I proposed it and then it happened."

"So, something supernatural, is that what you're saying?"

"Yes. Super plus natural."

"A man going around, shooting arrows, and people falling in love at his whim?"

"Yes."

"Sounds like a fairly egocentric fantasy."

"What? You weren't even going to talk to Jonah and now you're reviewing his resume like you're head of HR. And he's out there some place thinking about you so much his chest aches." That last idea temporarily won her favour. But then she put it all together and didn't like what it suggested.

She straightened up and away from him, as if she were about to address a cocky undergrad. "Life can offer glimpses of things that feel unique. You can find coincidences that make you think you're special for a while. Take my advice and keep them to yourself."

They walked home with decidedly less chat.

Despite the dressing down, Giordana's mood remained balmy and distracted. At a traffic light she bumped into a woman with a stroller. The stumble barely caused any shame, just a grinning apology.

Giordana kept putting her hands through her hair. Another symptom.

Sasha worried. As unknowingly as he had cast the spell, what if he could break it by making some other random gesture one day? Like once Giordana and Jonah were shacked up and knocked up. One morning, when Sasha tied his shoes the wrong way or gave the finger to a co-worker, the two lovebirds would wake up on their opposite sides of the bed to find that this supremely rose-tinted view had been stripped away.

Not that she would think to blame him for the abrupt

disappearance of her bliss. Scepticism of the outside world was her shtick, mainly because she had such fabulous belief in herself. She would spend the rest of her days looking inside for the answer. Her brain and heart, as far as she ever knew, were sound.

Belief in the function of one's brain and one's heart were basic tenets of life. The morning Alek first ran away, he woke Sasha so he could explain that fact in scattered, lengthy detail. He was tangential and sweaty – not in control of either, which went a long way towards proving his point.

"I'm leaving. Not forever, but I need to get out of here. Long enough to get my faith back."

He was too amped up about it all, the way he'd been ever since he'd quit school, to be intelligible. Sasha knew not to question his intention.

"I'm not telling you so you can tell them about it," Alek said. "No one could stop me anyway. I'm telling you because you're my brother."

Alek had no money and no social skills. Sasha guessed that the expedition would end with a police car in the driveway, bringing him home. Sasha swore secrecy and let him go. As Alek had said, no one was going to stop him. Even though they'd been living separate lives for most of high school, Sasha went to bed that night sad that he hadn't been asked to go along.

That next day at school, before their parents even knew he had left, Sasha felt sorry for his little brother. He pitied him for the brawl that was going to happen whenever he came back, and for being so sick in the head. Sasha remained true to his word though. That night and the next few days, as his parents slipped way past panic, he never confessed prior knowledge. Even when he himself began to envision darker outcomes. What was he going to do? He didn't know where Alek had been going anyway. Telling their parents would only have gotten Sasha into trouble.

The journey ended up taking three months. That didn't seem so long when you were grown up – time to pay off a mattress. But every day that Sasha kept his silence, he became more complicit in what he assumed was Alek's death, guaranteeing that Sasha would be left to play the good boy for his parents forever more.

The night Alek came back – using his key and calling out "hey," as if he had been to a movie – his parents screamed at him until they had rendered all of their fear and love. He said he'd spent a month at the beach and a month in the desert and a month in the woods, with a few other spots in between. He said he'd even stopped by the house a few times, but didn't feel like hanging out. Sasha had long given up trying to make sense of Alek's dreamy talk, but this pissed him off. He could have calmed everyone down with a single appearance. What drove their father crazy was the money aspect. How did Alek get by for so long? He said he coped. That wasn't sufficient. While their parents went off at him, Alek stayed mellow. At least he wasn't acting like the Messiah. His voice was calmer, smarter, as if he'd found what he'd set out for. All this relaxed talk made their parents more anxious, as if he were in a fugue state, and an even more unexplainable horror was right ahead.

The next morning Sasha woke up again to Alek sitting on his bed, tapping his feet too fast. Sasha tried to play it light. "You on your way again?" He vowed he would try to talk him out of it or at least make him say where he was going.

"No. I wanted to tell you: I know you're into guys and it's groovy with me."

Sasha was caught. At the word 'groovy', he felt as obvious and uncool as any teenager ever had.

"Thanks," was all Sasha managed.

"Every tree and every cloud says yes, be. We are not born onto this planet to judge each other, least of all our brothers. Got that?"

"Yeah." He understood. He would be quiet about Alek and Alek would be quiet about him.

Six years later, Sasha was driving an over-stuffed car with a futon tied to its roof, on his way to his first apartment. A pickup truck ran a red and sent him and the borrowed brown station wagon spinning back into the middle of an intersection at 5 p.m. on a workday. As if part of a perfectly-staged dance number, all the drivers on the road made it to their brakes in time, so that Sasha's car was left facing the wrong way, absolutely still amid a chorus circle of cars that had all stopped just short of collision. In that moment, as he pieced together the fact that he wasn't hurt, that there was no damage done, that he was invincible, the thought came to him that Alek hadn't sat on his bed that morning to blackmail him. Alek was trying to set him free.

Giordana nearly walked into another intersection.

Rather than putting his arm out to stop her, he said, "Is that Jonah over there?" She looked around and then at Sasha. Her expression showed irritation, then amusement. She was unflapped. If a downpour had started she would have burst into song and twirled an umbrella. What had Sasha done to her? Would she and Jonah disco onwards like this, hand in hand for fifty scintillating years of marriage?

Sasha didn't expect anyone beside his parents to be blessed with such longevity. They had clocked nearly forty years. A half-century, even six-tenths, would be a no-brainer. For the rest of the lesser beings, though, it was a quaint idea, like a comfortable pension. The institution was impractical. Of course, on your own, you still had to work at the loneliness, but you weren't stuck. There was the independence. If your stars aligned with someone else's, you could chirp about it for a bit, but in the end you were always free/alone.

Sasha and Alek had each mastered the independence part, but their stars had been uncooperative. Alek's situation was because he was, to give it a charitable frame, too much of a drifter. He could whine about unasked-for solitude all he wanted but few women – few humans over twenty, really – found perpetual wanderlust and sudden enthusiasms to be either amusing or cute. Alek said he was lonely, but he never held still. What did he expect?

Sasha's excuse was that he had found, to give it an equally charitable frame, regular outlets. These men – in the gym, in the produce section, wherever – provided exactly enough daily frisson to counteract nightly ennui. The thrill of the hunt, he believed it was called. The absence of anyone worth keeping.

Meanwhile, back in the suburbs, their parents sat comfy and warm in front of their gas fireplace, never saying a word to either of their boys about love. Whether Alek was able to secure a girlfriend was the least of their concerns about him. With Sasha, they seemed to know to keep themselves ignorant. They didn't pry and he wasn't about to enlighten. Aside from Damon's brief, early promise, Sasha never stayed with anyone savoury enough to bring home, so what would have been the point in making a big fuss?

Giordana's preparations for her afternoon delight were spectacular to observe. A professor dithering between a camisole and a T-shirt. She got off her high horse enough to engage Sasha to choose the perfume. He went with faintly woodsy.

The second she left, he got bored and called the blond from the night before. Sasha forgot the guy's name as soon as he was reminded of it. As a surer sign of devotion, Sasha made it into the shower and over to the apartment of whomever it was in half an hour.

There wasn't even a name on the buzzer. He couldn't ask again.

Party had prepped for sex by showering and then going for a run. His armpits tasted more like clean sweat than soap. This flavour was sampled right inside the front door. Sasha felt too tame for having showered, but the guy didn't seem to hate what Sasha tasted like, so their business evolved over to the sofa. They worked their way through the usual bases, flipping each other for agreeable access to the choicer regions. From the bedroom, their eventual destination, mid-period Madonna thrummed. Cheap soundtrack for a sunny day. Damon would have asked him to turn it off, but Sasha wasn't about to complain.

Their bodies fitted together. Party's strength met Sasha's solid frame, the blond faux-badboy buzz met Sasha's short brown ringlets. At one breather, Sasha indulged a poetic glance into his partner's eyes. They were actually a striking grey, if that was even possible. The colour was a field of smooth slate. It made his thoughts seem distant and tranquil – appealing.

Was this what he wanted? A piece who offered some peace? As a match they were reasonable. What if suddenly those grey pupils started shining for Sasha? What if he ended the endless search right there?

No, he was destined to be what he had always been, an amusing networker. Light diversion for the other folks living actual lives, while he flounced around like some eunuch. All right, not a eunuch exactly. And what if he tried to give himself and Party the depth charge and it only worked halfway? What if he felt nothing and was trapped forever with a sexy stalker? Or vice versa? It could get awkward.

Sasha had another look at the fringed pillow they were pushing against. It was new, not inherited. He noticed the lily-of-the-valley tea set in the corner, which also looked pristine. Sasha could understand the presence of some genuinely inherited granny decor, but to buy it? It would never work, not even if he was head over heels.

They ended up in the bedroom a few minutes later, Madonna still bleating – it was a greatest hits CD, no less – with Party's heels over his head. Perfect enough, though. A robust sex session on a weekday, the dry afternoon light shining in, and the promise that when it was over he could leave the vacant eyes, the fringe, the wrong music and all of it, and take himself home.

Giordana came in quietly a few minutes past eleven, as if she had breached curfew. Sasha looked up from filler on the net to watch her get some water. She drank and planted the glass back on the counter with a decibel too much noise. The Jonah energy had clearly dispersed itself.

She sat down in the comfy chair, adjacent to his desk, leaned back and folded her hands on her stomach. The vibe was definitely going in the direction of their old-time therapy sessions. Or she was pregnant.

After a pause, she spoke. "Well. My thesis statement is solid."

Sasha tilted his head for more information. None came. "That's breathtaking news," he said.

Ignoring sarcasm was another one of her strengths.

"When you work on a single project," she said, "you never fully understand what you're doing. Most of the time you're playing with blocks. You put things together and then you put them into the right order till they can stand up on their own. The basic shapes are known from the beginning. You can find yourself close to the final chapter and you may have constructed a major argument, but in the back of your brain you haven't quite entered it. No new knowledge has occurred. While you're struggling through all the necessary tasks, you're secretly waiting for a unifying theory to emerge that will allow you to inhabit the structure."

"Is Jonah going to be in the acknowledgements?"

She took another drink of water. "When your city is nearly wiped off the map, what does that leave you?"

"Damp?"

"It leaves you with less than nothing. I've never understood why someone would stay behind with nothing to call their own and all the rubble around. 'Better to have loved and lost' doesn't apply. *To have lost* is serious business. Why wouldn't you simply change your city, change your name, start over? An enigma.

"Well. It seems there are places in life – not necessarily physical – where moving on isn't an option. Not because you're trapped, but because that's where you find your foundation. It's where your life became viable. Visible. There's no choice but to stay." Giordana looked across to Sasha as she stood up. "*That's* how the date went. So thank you for everything. Cupid."

"I see." Not only was he going to score major with Ruth for having introduced them, but it would also give her and Natalie some fresh meat to chew on.

"I came to get my bags," Giordana said.

"So you're moving in together?"

"I'll stay a night or two. I need to finish the section I'm writing. He's got a big desk. We can share."

"This is not you, do you understand?"

"Who is it?" she asked, daring him to bring up any alternate theories.

"You don't know Jonah."

Giordana wasn't moved. "I'll stay here tonight if it's going to rile you so much, but I'm going back tomorrow."

"It's not that. What if this *is* a tickle? It can go away just as suddenly."

"Sasha. Duh. I am not only an adult, I'm an historian. It may not work out. Do you want me to sign a waiver so you don't feel liable? Here's what I'm telling you: you can rebuild your city but no one wants to live there; or they do want to live there but the crops are toxic; or the water is somehow still drinkable but the parks are haunted by a thousand ghosts. There are already a zillion reasons why every enterprise won't last. Why anything continues when all it should really do is fall in a heap is a mystery. In the end you may be the one who stays or you may be the one who goes, but this is where you are and you have no choice but to try."

~

The streets were filled with lovers. Sasha was the singlemost single person out there, like there'd been some sort of romantic pandemic and he'd been stuck below in a shelter. He sketched out a *Twilight Zone* episode, with him wandering the street, the last uncoupled man on the planet, searching, searching until he would finally meet the other loneliest man in the world and that would be—? Alek?

Sasha walked faster, counting the streets and keeping his eyes on the pavement.

There was a final pause at Damon's front door.

He had been the one to bail on Sasha with little notice or reason.

People made mistakes.

He was didactic about vegetables and recycling.

That didn't constitute an actual flaw.

He wasn't friendly with Sasha's friends unless he liked them himself.

Which Sasha admired.

He was capable of sitting and reading for hours on a weekday evening. He had focus that Sasha could only dream of. Damon could beat Sasha at Scrabble. And sexually, there were no complaints – though he was trying not to let that factor into the equation.

Damon opened the door, as if he'd heard him thinking about sex.

"Were you just going to stand there heavy breathing on my doorbell?" He was wearing torn tracksuit pants and no shirt. "You want a beer?"

"No thanks."

"Come in anyway. Catching up on dishes, three days' worth. I'm in the zone."

"No problem," Sasha said, following him through the cramped hallway into the kitchen.

If he did this, if it lasted, whose take would they get? Damon's first five minutes of connection, replaying on endless loop, or Sasha's picket fence fantasy? Or would it be bona fide, some forgiving view onto their ever-expanding hearts?

"Did you come by for a quickie?"

"A slowie, maybe."

From the sink, Damon gave him a sceptical glance.

The open CDs spilled onto a shelf by the stereo. The laptop, open to a sex site. Touching. The scraggly ficus Damon had taken from their place wasn't getting enough water. The painted tile they had bought together at a garage sale, a square of perfect blue that under any light wavered like a swimming pool, was propped against the wall, right next to the sofa. If anyone was careless, it could fall and crack. How did he get away with calling himself a perfectionist?

Damon watched Sasha's inspection. "You don't want a beer?"

"No, I'm all right."

"Are you certain about that fact?"

"Yes."

Damon returned to the dishes.

Sasha slowed down and looked at Damon's back. It was bare, still innocent. His face was at ease, engrossed in removing some carbonised gunk from a pan with his thumbnail, like it was the most important project in the world.

After buffing it to a polish, he rinsed the pan, turned off the water and shook his hands dry, wiping them on his pants. He turned them up, palms towards his face, like a doctor ready for surgery.

"Okay now. What can we do for you this evening?"

Peter

What you do with your grief should be your own business. You can weep if you like, but it won't make any difference. If you do, make sure it happens with decreasing frequency, until the departed doesn't cloud your presence at all. Sudden tears in a restaurant or excessive mention of their name, especially if you slip into the present tense, may cause discomfort among your loved ones. Friends – couples especially – stay away. Those who have survived similar loss hover around sickly. Most, however, find an apparent inability to let go depressing. After the sympathy is over, if you haven't moved on, the phone quietly stops ringing, as if you had died too. All in all, it's best to avoid discussion of your loss and, when asked, offer the appropriate lie: I'm fine. Anything more is what the kids call 'too much information'.

Natalie, whom Peter was thinking of in the present tense, once said that a person would have to be a witch or a wizard to keep from falling into a pit of sadness after losing their spouse. He had never imagined that she would go first, so he hadn't fully thought out his own grief before now. What was so surprising at the funeral that morning, where he cried so ferociously that only Ruth was brave enough to stand by his side, was how little he cared about anybody else. The funeral belonged entirely to him.

With Natalie buried just a few hours ago, he braced himself on the kitchen counter and allowed that it might be early yet. There were live people eating and drinking and talking in the next room. They were a relief. Anything so that he wouldn't be stuck alone with nothing.

After forty-one better-and-worse years together, Natalie had died of an unheralded aneurysm. There had been talk of a headache the afternoon of his birthday – his seventy-third – four days earlier. She hadn't thought much of it so neither had he. For dinner, they had gone to a new seafood place nearby, with white tablecloths and packets of crackers in the centre of the table. It was fancy enough for an ordinary birthday, but it was their last meal together and they had wine by the glass. They could have ordered a bottle. As soon as they were home, she said goodnight and went upstairs to sleep off the headache, while Peter stayed downstairs to read the next day's editorials online. Two hours later, he came into their bedroom and found her curled on her side, look-ing nearly comfortable, with her mouth hanging open at an odd angle. She was still and her colour had already drained away. In a sweat, Peter looked around at the dresser, at the door to their wardrobe, to see if the real Natalie was hiding somewhere, but when he looked back to her, he could see that she was completely as she was when he walked in. He didn't say her name. He touched her hand and it was cool.

Even after their dutiful attention to doctors' warnings, the brisk walks, medications in the morning, not to mention all the broccoli and grains, they were blindsided by this. It might have been avoided, their doctor casually mentioned, by a trip to the emergency room instead of up to bed.

One of Peter's tasks would be to concentrate on never replaying the evening again. And not thinking about her every time he entered the bedroom, or not tearing up every time he came home to an empty house. From this point onwards, his primary job was recovery. That required focus, he thought, involuntarily wrinkling his forehead. Natalie would have laughed at this twitch of intensity. The meaning between his brows was always clear to her.

Sasha came into the kitchen holding an empty platter. The living room door swung open behind him and the swells of conversation came in, the people who had come back to the house after the funeral. He heard Ruth, with her ever-effusive voice, saying, "She always wanted—" as the door swung closed again. Peter caught himself wondering what Natalie had always wanted. To avoid that line of thinking or, indeed, contact with anyone else who could lead him into tears, he started to rinse the dishes piling up in the sink so that there wouldn't be too many to do later.

He looked at Sasha, who was taking care of the things that Peter couldn't, and found himself thinking, *good boy*, as if his son were a dog.

"Dad. What's up?" Sasha took the sponge from his hand. "You're worse than me. Cut the cleaning. People are still here. They're not even slowing down. That ham is half gone. I can cut up more vegetables if we've got them."

Peter's hands rested on the ledge of the sink. He wasn't sure if there were any more vegetables. Natalie had brought some home from the market last week, but even if they were still in the house it wouldn't be right to serve them. One should not do the shopping for one's own funeral.

What was he going to do with the vegetables – let them rot until they turned into soup? Seal them in plastic for archiving?

"I don't know what's there," he told Sasha, who was already scouting out the pantry.

Peter didn't want to slice a carrot. Only Natalie would have known how angry he'd become. She had died. Where was Sasha's respect?

"Should I make a run to the shops?" Sasha said.

He thought, *Go away*.

And Sasha vanished.

Peter turned to see if he had walked around the corner into the pantry, but he wasn't there. The cupboards were all closed. Only the sound of the kitchen door, swinging to a stop. He pushed it open ajar to peer out into the living room. No one. No used plates stacked up on the table, no damp glasses abandoned without coasters on bookshelf ledges.

All he could see was the bouquet of yellow freesias from the couple across the street, which they had left on the front step that morning. They were younger than Peter and Natalie, by maybe five years. He imagined them putting the flowers down in a hurry and running away as if the house had been cursed. The freesias had ended up in a vase that was far too big for them. A milk bar condolence card was tied with blue twine to one of the stems. He hadn't unknotted it, so it rested against the vase. Natalie would have made it all look less pathetic.

Otherwise, the room was empty. The ham was wrapped, still in the box on the floor, in the spot he had left it when he brought it in from the car. Intact.

Bewildered, Peter paced the living room and front hall. No cars were parked on the street in front. He went back through the study and into the kitchen, too disturbed even to say Sasha's name aloud.

When the search proved futile, he picked up the phone and called him, expecting a ring to come from somewhere in the house. It didn't.

Sasha answered.

Peter asked, "Where are you?"

"I'm ten minutes away, I can still come back. What's the matter?"

"I'm fine," he said, not entirely convinced. "Listen. There's this enormous ham to eat. Any suggestions?"

Sasha laughed. "Dad, I tried."

"Did I resist?"

Sasha had no idea of his father's confusion. "A touch. You said you didn't want everyone coming over to feel sorry for you. You booted us all out."

Peter was unsure what was expected here.

"Look, I need to get home anyway so I can straighten out work tomorrow, but I'll be back for the weekend. Don't try to do too much. And don't snap at company if you need company. Call me whenever, any hour. And I guess you could freeze the ham. Or I'll come back and make pea soup. It'll be getting colder soon."

Peter signed off and put the phone back on the kitchen counter as if it were a strange instrument handed to him in a dream.

The sink was gleaming clean; untouched since the scrubbing he had given it at 5 a.m.

All of those people he'd sent away.

Come back.

Suddenly, the voices were there in the next room again.

Peter pushed the kitchen door open and walked out into the watchful love of family and friends. They all turned his way. The few tufts of snowy hair on his head, the thick, white eyebrows sprawling across his forehead in bewilderment. They would mistake it for simple mourning. Each in their own way was beckoning him over so they could console him for his loss.

He stood in the middle, trying to absorb it all. Ruth, laughing at something in spite of herself, streaks of tears on her cheeks. Her resemblance alone was hard to bear. Ivan's presence made it possible. He was interviewing Giordana and Jonah about life in Cairo. Youth in all its eagerness. Barely through his first semester and already drinking wine like such a sophisticate. Not a clue as to what else might come. Ben and Janelle were having heated negotiations with each other in the corner. The kid was nearly out of their house. What kind of conflict could be left to dissect?

Linda from across the street reflexively tidied up. A damp glass that had been left on a shelf was put onto a napkin. After being insistently helpful with all of the arrangements over the last two days, she pounced on him before any of the others could.

In the year or two after her husband had died, Peter had volunteered his services for any of her household repairs that didn't require a ladder. But she kept asking for favours long after, as if the offer had been a permanent arrangement – not a simple gesture of condolence. Peter took longer and longer to respond to her requests, until she got the hint. Since Tuesday, though, the story had changed again. She seemed to expect him to come to her aid, even now, as she pressed her hand against his wrist.

"What can I do?" she asked.

"I don't know." He moved away.

He was glad the people had returned. A gathering of friends, family and neighbours – what, maybe twenty, twenty-five people? A few crowded rooms and half a ham. It didn't seem like much for the end of a life, but it was enough.

And Alek, out there somewhere. The news would get to him eventually.

Sasha passed by, heading into the kitchen with another empty plate. Peter stopped him to say, "I'm sorry about the phone call."

Sasha looked confused. "What phone call?"

Awkward for a moment, Peter glanced at the white plate. It was worth a try. *Let's have some more vegetables?*

Instantly, the plate was loaded with celery, carrots, cherry tomatoes, and radishes cut into roses. Sasha looked down, not bothered at all by the sudden apparition. He said, "You want me to pass these around?"

Sasha hadn't even reacted.

Peter took his son's head between his hands, pleased, as he always was when he noticed Natalie's curls on his head. Even these, he saw, had a few strands of grey lurking in their midst, which comforted Peter with the only thing he was sure of: he was getting old.

An hour later, he stood in the driveway, accepting all the

goodbyes given with the extra urgency that comes after death. Holding Sasha again, he asked him not to come back until the next weekend, reassuring him that a daily phone call would suffice.

Before the sun had set, he tried to clean up from the gathering by asking for it. He was methodical, picturing how the house should look. As he formed the idea, he was sure to include the fact that the plates had been used by his visitors. He didn't want to accidentally disappear the afternoon from history. The house instantly cleaned itself, with the paper and plastic even appearing in the green bin by the back door. This was all extremely convenient.

The evening cool came on. Peter paused to look out from the screened verandah to the neighbours' houses, with their meaningless front lights and trimmed gardens. The house he was standing in looked the same as it did the week before. This was plain wrong. A flag or something should be at half-mast in front of the house from now on. He stood there, looking at the old floral sofa Natalie had found at the Salvation Army. It was deemed clean enough and cushiony enough. She helped him angle it in through the doorway. It would be an idyllic place for them to sit and read in their dotage. It would also keep burglars from thinking there was much of value inside. That was how she sold it to him.

The two of them rarely did read together, at least not as often as she had suggested. Peter always had other projects – sanding a table, planning a trip – that kept him elsewhere.

He wondered about the quiet hours they could have enjoyed had he found the time. When he was younger, he actually worried that they would be bored with all the years they had in front of them. As comfortable as the sofa looked, with its cushions mashed down by an afternoon of loved ones, he didn't see the point of sitting there alone.

Without even thinking concretely, he wished for Natalie to be sitting next to him.

She didn't materialise. Perhaps he wasn't being exact enough.

He wanted to trace her chin once with his forefinger, the way she used to do to him when she was trying to emphasise her side of an argument. He wished he could give her a life-saving massage: he would smooth the bubble of blood away, a fraction above her right ear, where her silver frizz had grown thin. Again, he focused on his goal, on the steady pulse of her body that was always somewhere in the house. Nothing. He didn't have to look around to know it hadn't worked. He tried again, this time less greedy, not trying to get rid of the aneurysm itself – accepting its existence as fated – but wishing that they had gone to the emergency room at the first twinge of a headache, that whatever treatment they had for her there had worked, that he might be holding her hand through months of rehabilitation. They would get through it. He looked around for even a shift in the air.

Nothing. All of it – the disappearing people, the reappearing ham – was merely his madness in grief.

He looked at his shoes. To prove he had been weaving reality with make-believe, he said to his laces, *Untie.* They did. *Tie.* He watched the transformation as they tied themselves up again, not slipping under and over each other into a knot, but suddenly pinching up like clay from a small tangle lying across his shoes into an upright and tidy bow. He thought he heard a sound and glanced back into the living room, looking for her, but all he saw was the freesias falling sparsely in their vase, with the card dangling down like a hanged man.

If he could will people to leave the house – to have left – it was reasonable that he could bring Natalie to the hospital in time. Nevertheless, as many ways as he phrased it in his mind, she did not appear. The more times he attempted it and failed, the more tired he became until he gave up. Rubbing his face to forget it all, he went to sleep on the sofa, cuddling up to a lavender-coloured quilt Natalie had made when the boys were small.

Peter accepted that this situation might be present for a while. It was probably an unspoken, unstudied condition that all widowers developed. He would keep their secret. After all, if he mentioned it to anyone, he would end up medicated. These were bearable delusions – as long as he didn't request the pleasure of his wife's company. It would be another thing to make peace with.

The new abilities enabled him to do the types of things she would have done if she were still there. He willed the books on the living room shelves to categorise and then alphabetise themselves within distinct categories. She had been talking about that one for years. A rip in the screen of the big kitchen window repaired itself in a blink. He thought of the foods that she had always wanted him to eat and they dutifully filed into the refrigerator and cupboards. Just as dutifully, he ate them. Natalie, who never understood his impatience with daily chores, would have enjoyed seeing him devote his gifts to getting the housework done. He could have considered grander wishes – say, a new car or money in the bank – but for what? For whom?

What he did do himself was make sure that he trotted the circuit around the reservoir in the early afternoon, while it was still light. For several days in a row, he made two complete loops, one hour and fifty minutes. Coming home through the streets, he forced himself to smile and say hello to everyone he passed. If Natalie had been there when he came home from these walks – she'd be reading on the verandah and vaguely waiting, forever fingering the next page of her book – she would have seen the blankness in his eyes and would have asked if he had enough time on his walk to worry about everything under the sun and still see that it was shining.

The evening before Sasha was supposed to visit, Peter invoked her roast pumpkin mash, which appeared fully seasoned, with thyme from the garden scattered across the plate as if by her own fingertips. As he sat down to eat it, he tried to hear her playing the piano, but the sounds never progressed from his mind to the living room. When he stumbled upon limits like this, it all felt random, sadistic. It made him long for this part of the mourning to be done. The pianoless silence made him lose his appetite and he made the meal disappear. He vowed not to think about any of her dishes again.

The visit from Sasha went well. He was certain that Sasha and Ruth were already in league, speculating about his ability to manage on his own. The order of the house provided conspicuous evidence of coping.

Sasha volunteered to make an initial sorting of Natalie's clothes. Peter stayed downstairs for most of this. When he did come up and saw her belongings being methodically transferred from the wardrobe into folded piles, and making their way into shopping bags, he had to sit down.

"Coming up the stairs must have made me light-headed," Peter said, fooling nobody. He stared at the stacks Sasha had made. How could Sasha even stand to touch her clothes as if they didn't even matter?

When his own father had died, when Peter was fourteen, their dog was shattered. There was no explaining death to Lila. She left food in her bowl and never settled. She barely seemed to sleep. Leaving the house for an errand or a proper walk was out of the question. She was up all the time, sniffing the corners of every room, looking around with a constant question on her face. It was a boiling hot summer and Peter's mother, who wasn't doing so well herself, needed relief from the pacing. She took his father's tan pyjamas and hung them out on the clothes line for Lila to smell, thinking it would get her outdoors at least. The top and the bottom were on two different hangers but, standing on the back step, you could almost make out his body in them. Lila stood right underneath them and just howled.

She went at it for more than an hour. Neighbours looked over the fence, but when they saw what was happening they pulled their heads back and kept walking. They knew. It was so bad that Peter's mother said they had to get away. She walked Peter into town to get an ice-cream sandwich. It was a relief. Years later, he still felt he shouldn't have enjoyed the ice-cream as much as he did, but it was the first pleasure he'd had in a week. When they came home, Lila was still under the clothes line, but she was cried out, asleep, curled up like she was at her master's feet. They got some peace after that. Less sniffing, less fretting. They thought it was out of her system. A few months later she dropped dead anyway, right on the pavement in front of the house.

Everyone knew your life in those days. The old vet told them that Lila died because Peter and his mother had to keep living. So they did. The pyjamas went into the right corner of the bottom of his mother's chest of drawers, hiding her few pieces of jewellery. The pyjamas stayed there until she died thirty years later and they had to empty out the house to sell it. Even after all that time, Peter couldn't touch them. Natalie could. Everything was going to the dump.

"What else are you going to do with your father's pyjamas?" she had asked.

The few times Sasha brought up Natalie's memory that weekend, he did so as if he were prying open a locked door on a cabinet. Peter and his son hadn't spoken much in recent years, so he recognised this for what it was and did his best to appreciate it. He indulged Sasha with murmured agreement about how happy his mother had been during those last months, how engaged she had been with her friends, and – subtlety was never the boy's strongest suit – how full a life she'd had. Peter permitted the talk, to a point, but he was concerned that some inopportune wish would intrude on their afternoon and something would happen. Natalie's long-imagined new kitchen would appear. Peter didn't want to be seen to be startled or unsteady.

Late Sunday, as Sasha drove away, Peter felt fondly towards the effort he had made. He willed his son to meet someone, someone he could relax and settle down with.

He understood that even if his wish worked that night, he wouldn't hear about it for months, unless Sasha told Ruth, and she, in turn, told Peter.

In small ways, Sasha seemed to cherish his selfishness as if it were a strength to be nurtured. He made jokes about it. Lord only knew how his housemate Damon got along with him for these past years. It was an enigma. But Peter was as bad, if not worse, when he first met Natalie. Her influence was the necessary spark that kept it from settling in.

During their first weekend away together, they camped on his grandfather's property. They would go boating at the pond. Peter had been talking about it for several weeks with his friends, as if none of them had ever taken a girl rowing. He would pack meals and show her the coves of his childhood. If it was warm enough, they would swim together and see what else transpired.

Instead, it rained. His disappointment made him cranky and untalkative all weekend. Everything he did, he did grudgingly. They drove back in silence. That Tuesday, he called and told her they weren't suited. He was sorry, but that was the way it was.

A few days later, he received a letter from her telling him he was wrong. She wrote that she couldn't have stopped the rain. It wasn't polite of him to rob her of happiness because of it. Moreover, she summarised, she had no backup plan if the letter failed in its mission. This meant that in order to get on with their life together, he would simply have to become the man she already knew him to be.

Peter had kept the letter in a folder on its own in his filing cabinet, as if it would one day be worth more than the others he'd kept – as if they wouldn't all end up going to the dump. When he first received her letter, he read it and dismissed it. The next day, he was reading the newspaper and looked up at the tree shedding its bark outside of his window and decided – the way you do when you're in your twenties and everything becomes blindingly obvious – that she was the one.

Peter found her note. Years had made the paper see-through and although he had remembered her words as having her usual certainty, this time he read in them a girlish heart, nearly broken and taking an enormous gamble. They had come close to not going any further. He closed his eyes and concentrated. He wished he had been smart enough to survive his doubts after that weekend nearly half a century ago. He wanted to spare her whatever pain he had caused for those days. He waited for the page to disappear from his hands into nothingness.

It was still there.

All he wanted was to undo one weak deed, but even this was not allowed. He went upstairs to bed.

If, as Natalie used to say, cleaning brought its own satisfactions, he did not find them. He let his sleeping self or the elves or whoever it was do the dusting, but otherwise he called on his power less and less. This way he wouldn't be so reliant on it when it went away. The shopping gave him a reason to see people, and cooking passed the time. What was he expected to do, sit still for the remaining years?

Invitations from neighbours offering temporary distractions were dutifully accepted. He resolved to embrace them while they were sincere. He pretended to be affable. He listened to what other people had to say and when asked, said, "It's hard, but I'm getting there."

Linda came over one night and roasted a chicken. It seemed like a friendly enough gesture when she offered. Besides, he was tired of sitting at the table by himself. Then she was there, opening drawers to find wooden spoons, yammering about the logic of kitchens. She was trying it all on.

They didn't talk about her dead husband and they didn't talk about his dead wife. What was there to say? She tried to engage him in discussion about the house going up on the corner and what an eyesore it would be. Peter had talked to the workmen and told her that the next step, the rendering, would improve it. That was one topic. She started another. An all-drum orchestra would be performing at the arts centre the next month. ("They were amazing. We saw them when they came through here last time." No comment was made about that 'We'.) Linda was going to buy tickets, if he was interested. He told her he might be. That was another topic.

He washed and she dried. Fighting it was useless. If she hadn't invited herself over, they would have been pushed together in some other way. In the alchemy of the neighbourhood, a level of attraction between two half-empty homes like theirs was a given.

Peter hurried the clean-up along so the evening would be over. With nothing left to do and no offer of a nightcap, Linda left before nine, waving her hand from over her shoulder as she went down the front steps, leaving no chance for even an uneasy pause. Glad to have the house back to himself, Peter admitted he had needed the company.

The deepest solace was the garden, which he kept in a permanent red and orange of late summer blooms, Natalie's favourite. He didn't have the nerve to go and sit there alone, but he enjoyed watching it from the kitchen. Knowing it was out there.

Sasha called daily. They had already settled into their new dialogue, which consisted of a steady, haphazard discussion of national news, chores related to Natalie's death, and finances. *Surface*, Peter thought, but he couldn't see a way to get underneath it, the way that the rest of them did. That's what Natalie was for. Every pause and sigh and "I wonder—" that she pressed into their conversations slowed things down to a reflective pace that after seventy-four years still eluded him.

Janelle called with the number of a local grief group that met every Tuesday. Peter could picture it: some big-eyed facilitator, desperate to connect with a seated circle of men exactly like Peter, each one mute without his interpreter, each suspended in his own amber past.

Natalie was wrong. Even though he had become some kind of wizard, he was still very sad.

Ruth said she would come by to see how he was doing. When he told her, "Come for lunch," it felt like a positive step. Though they had never had reason to speak much – again, that was Natalie's job, and he had long accepted a slight adversarial component in the sister-in-law role that was beyond anyone rectifying – she was close to Natalie in temperament and instinct.

Peter sliced bread at the low table in front on the verandah, when he saw her pull into the driveway. Watching her reach into the back seat of her car with a spry twist, she looked more like Natalie than usual. His skin went prickly. It wasn't until she waved at him through the window that he was relieved to see Ruth's fuller cheeks and more sceptical eyes. Already, he wouldn't know what to do if Natalie suddenly appeared.

She walked up the path carrying her customary foil-wrapped orange cake. Did she give them to her clients too? One day soon he would have to tell her that Natalie was the only one who had ever eaten them. It tasted good to them because it was their mother's recipe.

When asked on the front step, he was at a loss to describe how he'd been since the funeral. He wanted to tell her about the senseless power because Ruth might understand why it had come and how long it would last.

All he managed was a wordless shrug and tears. Ruth wrapped her arms around him and, thankfully, took over.

"Me too, my dear," she said, and put the foil package down next to their feet on the concrete. Her embrace was weaker than Natalie's would have been, but it would do. She didn't try to lead him inside. He looked over her shoulder at the other homes on the street. The cars in their mindless driveways. Peter wanted everyone to see. This was better than a flag. This is the time when you stand on the front step of your house and cry. He wanted to be like Natalie and Ruth, to express things this way with everyone. He wanted to be the person Sasha called first. He wanted to go to the grief group and wail through a year of Tuesdays until he understood everything about all of them.

He wished for it.

Over lunch, Ruth gently suggested a book on the grieving process that Peter might find useful.

"I would love to see it," he said.

"I didn't expect you'd jump for it. It's in the car."

"Why not? I'm curious. I've got the time."

Watching her retrieve the book, he thought about her review of a symphony that a friend had recently taken her to. Her simple use of the word 'conductor' brought up an incident that he hadn't thought about in years. When she came back and put the book on the table in front of them, he had to tell her.

"Our worst argument," he said, "was right after we married. We were still in the house on Banyan Street. I have no idea what it was about. I had evidently committed an act of bossiness. I could see I was in the wrong so I apologised as fast as I could, but it wasn't good enough. She said to me, 'Remember, my friend, you are not the conductor of my life.' I knew she meant musical, not train, but it hurt. I remember trying to feel better about it, that it was her way of reminding me that she didn't need me to live, which was a point that she needed to get across. But a decidedly unromantic statement to make to your new husband. There are so many times these days when I see how she was so definitely the conductor of my life. I don't understand why she would have said such a thing. What else could we have been for each other?"

Ruth tilted her head. Had he said too much? Even as he waited for her comment, he realised that she wouldn't have anything to add.

"The heat of the argument," Ruth said. "You meant

everything to her. That's not remotely sufficient, but you know what I mean. You had a good life together, whether you were conductors or not."

Peter let the answer sit there between them. It wasn't sufficient. No answer could be. Surely Ruth had questions from all these years of sisterhood. Questions could be a kind of inheritance too.

"Thank you," he told her, "I know, but it's still good to hear it said out loud." After a helpless pause, he asked, "Are you up to braving the task of going through a few of her clothes?"

In the upstairs guest room, Ruth rested her arm on the bed so she could lower herself to the stacks that Sasha had made. She sifted through the bags while Peter watched. He wasn't as upset this time. Was it because he'd been here once before?

Ruth wrapped herself in Natalie's pale blue cardigan, saying, "I always loved this, but I don't know if I could stand to wear it."

Peter nodded once, to let her know that it was all right if she did. Natalie used to put it on for gardening. It mystified him, but she always managed to keep it spotless. Would he be able to stand it if Ruth wore it till it was stained and moth-eaten? If she didn't take it, could he let it go to the Salvation Army – that recycler of lives? Yes, yes. He tried to consider it all. The clothes were there, they were connected to Natalie, but they weren't her. He saw each garment in crisp detail. They didn't make her her, any more than Peter had – or any more than she had made him him. Peter had not been her conductor and Natalie had not been his. This was the clarity he had been waiting for. You live your life adjusting the notes, meddling with tempos. You silence the brass, chase crescendos, but only you get to be the conductor. They had stood next to each other on different podiums, waving their little sticks for all those years.

This was why he couldn't bring her back. It was as if the power itself had come to underline this point: that it was his life to master. The thought that they were truly different people didn't depress him now. No, it made his mind rise, excited that they had stayed in tune for as long as they had. They had done well.

He wanted to tell Ruth all of this, but she was immersed in clutching every item to keep her sister close. *She's confusing emotions with materials*, he thought, newly enlightened. On impulse, he thought a treat might distract her from this project, or at least console her.

"Would you like some fresh peaches?" he asked.

She looked up, baffled by the suggestion. "What? Where would you get those at this time of year?"

"I don't know where they come from, but here—" and by simply opening his palm he created a plate of sliced peaches, pale pink and sweet. The power was still with him.

Unstunned, she put down a blouse and tried a slice, saying, "You must have had to hold up a bank to buy these."

"How about another wish?" he asked, with a child's glee in his eyes, "What would you like more than anything?"

"I'd like to not be rifling through Natalie's clothes," she said. "I'd like my sister back."

"That's not an option. I've tried," he said. "But I can help with the first one. Come with me to the garden."

And they were in the garden.

The sun was already behind the house, but the air hadn't begun its nightly chill. Ruth went along with the change in scene. She crouched over, pinching some ivy that had crept through the fence from the neighbour's yard. "There. You don't want this popping up," she said, as she tore it into tiny pieces.

Peter looked at her oblivious face. As far as she knew, they had come downstairs and out through the kitchen. Back upstairs, the clothes would be partially sorted whenever she went back to them. As far as she knew, a garden at the beginning of winter, or this garden at the beginning of this winter, would still be lush and in flower. It wasn't inexplicable to her.

This was how it worked: the things that were, this was the way they had always been. There was no convincing anyone otherwise. You were responsible for yourself, for what you had done. Enjoying that ice-cream sandwich was part of his life. Taking Natalie to the emergency room or buying a bottle of wine that night, or going rowing in sunshine that first weekend was not. To spend time in those places made up by regrets was folly. Wishing for them until they were distinct as memories, wouldn't make them true. He could mull over the alternatives for the next twenty years, shuffling and reshuffling, but it wouldn't touch what had been real between them. His pig-headedness, done; the afternoons they didn't spend reading together, done; every mistake they made with Alek, done. And not to be undone.

It was like being absolved. It was like being held up to the sky.

The first person he wanted to tell was Natalie. The crush of remembering her came and went a little faster this time. She wasn't there. Wherever she was, he was sure she would have been proud.

He had been too self-absorbed these last few weeks. He wanted to call Sasha and hear how he was doing since his mother died.

Where did he put the number for the grief group? The men there would understand.

"She was so in love with this jasmine," Ruth said, running her finger over a dark shiny leaf. "I'm sure it would take over my garden, but I'd love to have a cutting. Would you mind?" she asked, grabbing a sprig.

"Of course not."

He was distracted by the thought of his singular history, as if he had finally discovered a place to keep it. He glanced over the fence at the dried leaves in all the other yards around and felt irresponsible. *We need to catch up.* The jasmine would wither if he let the seasons in, but in a few months it would come back, whether he was there or not. With Ruth's cutting, it would continue somewhere else, maybe even take over.

"Let me get the clippers," he said.

Walking over to the low ledge by the house where Natalie kept her tools protected from the rain, he started to wonder what he would do after Ruth left. The question dissolved and he didn't even notice.

This was new, Peter without a plan. He was thinking about jasmine, wondering why its fragrance was so overwhelming in the evening. What insects were around to be attracted after dark when the air was so cool? One night he would sit out in the garden and watch. What an excellent idea. He picked up the clippers, snipped them twice at the air to make sure they hadn't started to rust, and headed back to the centre of the garden. Here, finally, was the man Natalie had married.

Alek

What was up with these kids? They were making him edgy. The girl was rocking in wide circles, pushing into her brother with each rotation. A wire snaked from her ear to her back pocket. The boy stared ahead, stiff. He wasn't about to let himself be distracted from his fierce watch over the traffic circle. It was like they were hanging out for pickup too, bags at their feet, anxious about some new chapter about to start.

The kids' faces didn't show the ease of a spring holiday. They were being sent away because of a divorce or a death. They were in the middle of a downgrade. As soon as their lift appeared, they'd be okay; Alek was the opposite.

It was the bus station's fault that he was thinking like this. The stains on the pavement, the empty sky. Leaving Technicolor for this black and white day was taking a toll. The any-second-now arrival of his own family, he had to admit, was part of the equation too.

A minor adjustment would lift things. He put cobalt-blue ceramic planters by each doorway to the station. He planted gardenias in some and camellias in the others. He made the plants grow bigger, swiftly pressing them from bud into flower. Their fragrance would wisp to the brother and sister, providing the mildest sedative effect. The visual shift wouldn't lead to any repercussions. It would be for his benefit alone. The boost for the kids might make them face their future with strength. It also might mellow him out.

The boy pushed the girl away. "Stop play-ing!" he said, stretching the word as far as it would go.

Alek couldn't keep himself from adding to the scene. He filtered the music from the girl's pocket through the station's sound system so that everybody could hear. It was outrageous to play anything stronger than 'Yesterday' in a public place, but he chanced it – the harder rock corner of the White Album. Two women in suits with wheelie bags chugged by, one of them turning her head in tune with the guitar riff.

The sister took out her earpieces and continued bopping. Her brother even joined in. They looked like two kids who had gone off on an adventure and were returning, full of tales to tell.

That was better.

Every journey had an invisible midpoint. Of his, Alek could see the first part. The people who were warm, the people who weren't. The haphazard decisions he'd made on the way; the ones he'd stuck with, the ones he changed. At some halfway point, though – not in miles or time, but in some other material – he started to leave where he was and come back to his family.

His parents, sitting peaceably on the screened verandah, turning pages in harmony. Ruth with her aqua-aerobics, teaching the Twist at the senior end of the pool. Sasha and Damon, hosting a bridge night. He lingered in their space, as silent and curious as any voyeur. The urge to fiddle with their lives had disappeared. He was content to just watch. After each trip, when he returned to visibility and whatever new home he had found, nothing seemed as real as where he'd been. Home always waited, solid. His travels away from them had only been a short walkabout.

Then the call from Giordana came.

"Enough. You've been gone too long. It's time for a visit."

Alek confessed, "I'd love to see you."

"I would love to see you too. And so would your parents. If only for a glimpse."

"I'm happy," he told her.

"I believe you, but people like to witness these things for themselves. People like me. You don't even know Jonah."

After that, the trip back was one straight stroke. The six-hour bus ride to the city, the three flights and two passport stamps, followed by one more bus from the airport to arrival bay fourteen and, finally, this bench.

The brother and sister were still fidgety, but definitely more chilled than before. He could look at them and believe their lives were settled. They were returning from camp or a visit to a favourite aunt. His little touches had made the difference. The feeling let him imagine that his whole trip would turn out to be one big beautification project.

No. What if their parents arrived and saw their son and daughter so relaxed? What if it gave them a pang? What if it altered the way they treated them?

This was why he had to be careful. One ripple pushed into another. Without even intending it, there would be waves, curling larger and larger, pulling all of them far from solid land.

In a blink, he stripped away the planters and turned the music all the way down.

Alek had to leave things as he found them. That was his condition for this trip.

In a few minutes, his family would be there and happy to see him. The feeling would be mutual. That was all that was required for the day.

The old tan Toyota pulled up to the traffic circle. His father drove slowly, scanning the benches, not sure exactly what he was looking for. Alek had to remember that they hadn't seen him in years. He had left at twenty-nine. He had become forty-one. What would they see?

On the bus from the airport, he had switched his drawstring pants for chinos, just for them. He had shaved downwards then upwards, the way his father taught him. There were distinct creases on his face, but these couldn't be helped. It would remind everybody of the passage of time. After they took in the superficial, they would be anxious to see if he was all there. His conversation had to be coherent. That meant keeping reality continuous. No meddling.

His father parked at an odd angle to the kerb and, with minor exertion, got himself out of the car. He stood in the road beaming and waving at Alek. His mother struggled to get out of the passenger seat, using her strong side to guide the weak side. It was still so hard for her, even after all the rehab. She had been tireless, doing every exercise she'd been given, whatever they told her to do. When he saw her face he was glad he had stepped in that time.

Two months had already passed when Sasha's letter found its way to Alek, telling him that she had died. He was touched to see the familiar handwriting on the envelope. Like the invisible visits back there, the letter provided another satellite signal, however faint and flickering, to guide him home.

In it, Sasha apologised for the delay and for sending anything as last century as a handwritten note. It wasn't the kind of thing he could put in an email though, and there didn't seem to be a reason to rush bad news. There was Sasha's ever-critical eye on their mother's pitiful funeral. The stranger with hay fever who presided, and the pointless gathering at home afterwards. Aunt Ruth had played the host while Dad stayed in the kitchen fretting about how much everyone was eating. Sasha suspected their father was taking some potent anti-depressant and denying it. Giordana, he also reported, had gone quiet. Worst of all was Ruth, who shrank overnight into an old woman. She had stopped her practice, stopped everything. There were only fragments left. Sasha said he barely considered himself to have a family. Their mother had orphaned them all.

There had been many, many pledges to not tamper, but Alek went back there – to his parents' house on the afternoon of the stroke, when the blood was still pooling in her brain. They were bringing groceries in from the car. His father put a new bag in the bin while she put a dozen items away, reaching into the fridge and the cupboard. Every gesture demanded and received the cooperation of her body. Alek followed her out of the kitchen and upstairs to their bedroom, wondering if he would be able to get it right. In the bathroom, she washed and patted her face dry. The clear box of cotton balls, the smell of the cucumber cleanser on her skin.

She paused and pressed her fingers high against her temples. It was starting to hurt.

Alek interfered. He took the heels of his hands and banged them once into the sides of her head. She might have collapsed right there and his would have been the last touch she would have known. The cotton ball fell from her hand into the sink as her hands went back to her temples. The surprise subsided and turned to worry. She inspected her face in the mirror, pulling at her mouth, staring at her pupils. Massaging her neck didn't make the concern go away. This was the effect Alek had wanted. The pain was a mere pearl at that moment, but she went downstairs and reported the jolt. His father insisted they go directly to the hospital.

"If we get it checked out and it's nothing, that will be a happy enough evening," his father told her as they reversed out of the driveway. She rested her hand on top of his. Both sides of her were still good. She said she loved him for giving up his birthday dinner to spend it being ignored in an emergency department.

Alek stood on the steps as they drove off. What had he done to their history? Sasha's letter was to report she had died, not to ask for help. The consequences shot in all directions like a Roman candle. If the trip to the emergency room went well, Sasha would get his mother, Ruth would get her sister, and Giordana, her aunt. His father's suffering would be erased. All that his father had gained from Alek's gift would be deleted too. Plus, there was the knock-on effect that altered everyone around them. Who else was on their way to the hospital that day? Who would lose out because of this woman and her stroke?

That half hour, watching his mother walk from room to room until they drove off – that was the midpoint of his journey. That's when he began to return.

A maroon sedan pulled up in front of the boy and girl on the next bench. An arm ushered the kids into the back seat as they dragged their bags across the kerb. Alek could no longer tell where they had been or where they might be going.

His parents were standing and waiting for him. Had he paused too long? He didn't want questions of his mental fitness puncturing the day. In five steps he was next to them. His mother crushed herself against him.

"It's been such a long time." Her errant, erratic son.

"I know." His once-deceased mother.

"Wonderful, wonderful," said his father, wrapping himself around the two of them.

Alek was home. That meant the sleepy confidence of his father's flannel shirt and his mother's damp, urgent embrace. It meant their happiness to hold him and the doubt that the calm would last.

Alek looked down and noticed a tear on the pocket of his mother's shirt. Home also meant the place where he saw what needed to be done. He remembered standing on a chair in the kitchen one morning before school while she sewed up the pocket of his shirt. To keep him still, she told him a story about an elephant's trunk that had become a thread and wanted to grab his nose. By hooking it through his shirt, she was trapping it there and saving his nose. She had probably stitched miles of patches.

What could be the harm in a little mending? He knew the

answer. If he wasn't careful with even a small fix like that, there could be a flood of other facts that would alter the landscape. Everyone else would happily inhabit the new world. Only Alek would be stuck in the one that came before. Too often he would slip up and refer to another scene that they knew had never happened. Who wouldn't want to medicate that?

They eased their hold on him as he forced himself to forget the unfairness of the tear on her pocket.

His father tested the weight of Alek's pack. "Is this all you brought?"

"It's all I own."

"Ah," his mother said, "Yes. 'Travel lightly'."

She glanced at a picnic table on a square of lawn. A couple was setting up for lunch. On the grass next to them, an infant slept in a bundle of blankets.

Alek's mother sighed and said, "We're very glad you're here."

His father said "Wonderful" again, as if no one had heard the first time.

The car radio was permanently set to public radio. An upbeat version of "Danny Boy" came on, with some woman singing slowly, full of bravery for whomever it was going off to fight, like war was a good thing. Alek asked his father to turn it up.

"Can you still sing?" his mother asked him.

"Don't be silly. Naturally he can still sing," his father said.

"I still sing."

"Will you do us the honour?" she asked.

Alek obliged, slowing down to the tempo the song deserved.

But come ye back, when summer's in the meadow
Or when the valley's hushed and white with snow
'Tis I'll be there, in sunshine or in shadow—

His mother sobbed once, loudly.

Alek listened.

She thought it was too late for him, coming back now. Some stupid accident in his brain, the damage that Peter and she had done, the drugs he had taken, the drugs they had forced on him, and the equally poisonous culture that they lived in. All of them were stuck in this violent mess that wasn't worth its pretensions of civilisation.

He stopped listening.

"Go on, go on," she said to Alek, not even pretending to control herself, and grabbing her bag for a tissue. "We haven't heard your voice in too many years."

Alek did, but it wasn't the same. "And if you come, when all the flowers—" and gave up, fading out to the sound of her gulping air. He reached forwards to put a hand on her shoulder. She shook her head for him to take it away.

His father turned off the radio. This was the right

soundtrack for the drive. They drove on like that, passing the university and the park where he and Vicenta used to make out. His mother wiped her face and slowed herself down with a few big breaths.

"It's nothing. I needed to do that. I'm all right now."

They pulled up the driveway. A crow hopped across the lawn towards them.

"Does the house look the same?" his father asked.

It looked neglected.

Alek said, "The same as it was, older than it was. Like each of us, I guess. Don't you ever walk into a room and get the feeling that you're old and young at the exact same time?"

"Hmm."

In the rear-view mirror, he saw his father's disappointment. Their boy was still odd.

"Dad, really? Not even when you get on a bicycle? You throw your leg over the bar, and even if you've done it a thousand times, every now and then you wonder if your leg will reach, if you're tall enough yet to ride."

"I'm sorry. I don't know what you mean." His father leaned forward, tightening and releasing his grip on the steering wheel. "Alek, I know you're probably in a hurry to see everyone. They all wanted to come to the bus station. Two cars' worth of family, but I said no. It's too much."

"Why? This is what I came back for. The whole pig pile."

"We don't want to wear you out on your first day here," his father said.

"You shouldn't call it a pig pile," his mother piped up, recovered enough to reprimand. "It's love. It's concern."

"Enough concern," Alek said.

"You're used to more solitude, is what she means," Peter added. "Your nomadic ways must have agreed with you or you wouldn't have stayed away so long. We don't want to jeopardise what you've accomplished."

"I haven't been living in a monastery. I'm not sick. I'm not recovering. I'm visiting – that's all." He tried to keep his voice level. The crow flew off, which felt like a judgement.

"Right, good," his father said. "The others are at Ruth's. We can call them immediately or call them later. Whatever you wish."

"Whatever I wish," he repeated. It was like they had never stopped fighting. He hadn't made any mistakes, but all they knew was that he was still not all right.

His mother pulled her left hand onto her lap and dropped her head back against the seat.

His father said, "Why don't we go inside and not let feelings run away with us?"

The house needed work, the kind of tasks his father was too old to start and too cheap to pay anyone to do. During the weeks after his mother's death, all of them had been put right. In exchange for these few more years together, though, the house had lapsed back.

The droop in the roof, the screen on the verandah and the broken gutter — Alek couldn't help himself — he fixed them. These were small favours, he rationalised. He was specific. Each change was discrete, unconnected to any person or action. There were to be no potential consequences of them living in a spruced up home. The upgrade wouldn't alter anybody.

"The house looks good, Dad," he said.

"We do what we can." His father kept his eyes on the path in front of his feet. The front garden was in a similar state of lovelessness. Again, keeping his parameters clear, Alek weeded, mowed, and put in dahlias.

His parents took their time with the five steps up to the front door. This was a project in itself.

"Are you all right?" he asked his mother as she used her right arm and right leg to balance her climb.

"You didn't see me just after. The physio says my range of movement is superb. I need to reschedule her. Don't let me forget." Out of breath, she leaned heavily against the handrail to conquer the last step. "You missed it. We

slept in the living room for the first year. But I perse-
vered. I can go upstairs on my own again now. A regular
Olympian."

Alek's first memory was of the kitchen. Aunt Ruth was
washing him in the sink. There was a baby-blue counter,
tiling all around and bright orange measuring cups floating
next to him. Ruth scooped the water up with one of the
cups and sprinkled it on his shoulders. He had never known
a more ecstatic pleasure. With infant logic, he wanted her
to feel what he was feeling. Reaching for the cup's handle
so he could pour water onto her, he fell forward. All babies
slip, no big deal. His face didn't even dunk. But the house
spoke to him: *you are not ready*.

He came up in tears, red and choking, the sort of
screams that terrify an adult. Ruth grabbed him away from
a monster she couldn't see. She had him out of the water
and close against her shoulder in an instant.

This was the current that ran through the walls from
then on: *you are not ready*. You are learning to walk – *not
ready*. You are going to school – *not ready*. You have important skills to master – *not ready*.

For the first few years Alek listened and held himself
back. He did as he was told, he played quietly, and he
didn't speak until spoken to. Although he heard his

parents discuss ways to improve his confidence, they agreed that fate had delivered them a very well behaved little boy.

Until one specific Saturday. Alek and Sasha were watching cartoons. There was a house on TV that kept turning lights and appliances on and off, whenever it felt like it, driving the family nuts.

Alek asked his brother. "Does our house ever say things to you? Does it ever bother you?"

Without taking his eyes from the screen, Sasha said, "No, the house doesn't pick on me at all. But the garage told me it hates your guts."

At dinner that night, Sasha ratted him out to their parents because he thought the question was funny. Their parents didn't laugh. Alek ran upstairs and they followed. Under the blanket on his bottom bunk was as far as he could get from them in those days. His father hovered over him, pulling the sheet away from his face to ask if what Sasha had reported was true.

"Yes."

His father straightened up tall and assured him, "Well the house doesn't talk. To you or anyone. That's that. Understood?"

Alek nodded.

"He's a big boy. He'll right himself," Alek's father said as he left.

"Can I stay a bit longer?" Alek's mother asked him.

Lingering usually meant that she wanted to soften whatever his father had done, so he let her close the door and come sit next to him on his bed.

"Do you hear the house?" he asked, hoping for a yes.

She put on her teacher voice. "For an imaginative boy like yourself it can be hard to tell the difference between real and make-believe—"

"Go away."

"—when we hear stories – especially ones that make us happy or make us scared, or make us feel any of our feelings – it's easy to get caught up. Sometimes they're about remarkable events and they make the everyday world make more sense. They can even tempt us to spend more time away from our own—"

"Please. Leave! I'm asking!"

"I'm going." She stood up and left.

The bedroom door slammed after her, like in the cartoon house on TV. The house must have heard him tell the others of its existence. It wanted him to know how mighty it could be. Alek cried into his bed, like he had into his aunt's arms, but sucking back tears to stay as quiet as he could. He didn't want the house to think it had beat him. All evening he curled up in a corner of the bed, trying to still his breath, mastering it so well that the covers didn't even move.

Downstairs, Sasha fell asleep over a jigsaw puzzle and their father carried him up to bed. Alek pretended to be sleeping but he opened his eyes in time to see Sasha's legs floating up to the top bunk.

Their father gave Sasha a kiss and said, "Good night, little man upstairs." For a thousand bedtimes before, whether they were asleep or not, this was followed with a kiss to Alek's forehead and "Good night, little man downstairs." That night he skipped Alek. He wasn't willing to take the risk of waking this peculiar little boy. That was the first bubble of special treatment. Later, its diameter would expand exponentially, insulating him from them and them from him, but that night it was already the size of the solar system.

His father left the door ajar, as usual, to let light in from the hall.

Alek looked angrily at his father's shadow in the hall, *I don't need your stupid bathroom light.*

The door closed.

Alek shook. *I want the light back*, he thought, and the door swung to its previous angle.

He was the one doing this.

From then on, the house and its inhabitants weren't so scary. He started with the doors and windows and went on from there. The walls that had been his enemies became his friends.

Alek wanted to know more about this thing that had scared him. He tailed his father, demanded the meaning of every word and every thing he could think of. He competed with Sasha whenever he could, at first fixing every game so he would win, then only fixing every other game, so Sasha would continue to play. Alek practised and perfected. He learned moderation about his skills and caution against unimagined consequences. Invisible, he hung around in the kitchen while his mother talked on the phone to Ruth, discussing the secrets of their family and the many ways that Alek was blossoming.

He heard himself called enchanted, imaginative, sensitive, extravagant, wild, wilful, distracted, distant, absent, troubled, delusional, psychotic. The way Alek saw it, he was coming into his own.

It was Vicenta, his first love, who helped him to understand how he got this way. The two of them were on her mother's bed smoking her mother's dope. A week of autumn rain had led them to discover the stash.

"Where do you go off to when you ditch school?" she asked.

He had learned to travel by then. He went everywhere but he was always home by dinnertime. "I don't know."

She bonked him with a pillow.

"Fine. It's your personal life. At least tell me why you gave up swimming? You used to love it."

He was in the mood to confess. He usually kept this

kind of thought to himself, but they were lying side-by-side, high, and she was playing with his earlobe. "The water fights me," he said.

Vicenta had to sit up so she could laugh properly. She braced herself on his hip, rocking the bed with closed-eyes hysterics.

"You fight the water," she said when she stopped cracking up. "The water doesn't fight you. That's how you learn to swim: you stop fighting. And, to be crystal clear, that's a metaphor. Do you know what a metaphor is? I don't want to see you throwing any punches in the shower."

"But I don't have gills, I don't belong there. The water doesn't want me there."

"You, my friend, must be a brand new soul," she said, tapping a finger on his forehead. "In your cosmos, every little flower has a goddamn feeling."

"Not *every* flower."

"Okay, but if you have trouble with something it's because that something's against you. Am I right?"

"I'm not paranoid."

"Nobody said you were. But you give inanimate objects emotions. Can we admit to that?"

"Water isn't inanimate," he said.

"It's water. It doesn't care about you, it doesn't care about itself. It spends its days trying to find its own level, that's it."

"Then shouldn't I stay out of its way?"

"When I said 'trying' I didn't mean that the water wants

anything." She covered her eyes with a hand, laughing more. "Talking to you sometimes, mister. It's like you just got here."

Finally, something made sense: he was new.

The idea comforted him and he drummed the mattress with pleasure. His enthusiasm amused Vicenta and she scratched his head. He licked her hand and she gave up, scratching his stomach like he was a dog. He burrowed around her hips in a squirmy celebration. She had explained his universe with one little thought.

He wanted to reward her. It had worked with Giordana and he was sure he could do it again. With a few breaths, he spread himself into an X across the quilt, nearly pushing her off the bed. He concentrated. She should have a constant flow of clear thinking. A scientific mind that would allow her to discover whatever she wanted. With her wisdom nearby, she would always tell him what was really up.

When he opened his eyes she looked exactly the same as always, face open and doubting, watching him for signs of presence.

"What was that? Why'd you trance out on me?"

Three days later, she announced that there was no future for them as a couple.

"There's always going to be two separate paths for us," she said like she'd been practising it. "I'm sure it's totally obvious to me and totally not to you, but that difference right there is how it would be for us. You thinking one way and me the other, forever."

Alek had not only given her something she didn't need, he had brought this all on himself. Helpless, they sat there and started their long goodbye, on the front steps of his house, just out of the way of the rain.

The hallway was sagging and chipped, much like his parents. The afternoon would be punctuated by creaks. Some easy, pretty touches might improve moods and flexibility.

No, too risky. Instead, he restumped the foundations. Subtle, but lasting. The house would stand as long as they needed it. He got ahead of himself and before he knew it, the leak he could hear in the kitchen wall was taped, every room was repainted, and the floors were sanded from a dull tarnished bronze to goldenrod, right under their feet. It's just a visit, he reminded himself.

"So Alek," his father said, resting his hands heavily on his shoulders, "why don't you get settled."

Alek dropped his pack in the middle of the front hall. "Done."

His father smiled, a bit more easily than before. Maybe there had been an effect from the renovations. "Then may I give the others their marching orders?"

"I'm all geared up for the love and concern pile."

"Will do." Content with a job, his father headed for the kitchen.

Again, his mother embraced him as best she could, resting her head against his chest. "I'm never letting go," she said.

He looked around for other touch-ups he could do. The time that he had admitted to Vicenta that he once believed the house to be a force of evil, she didn't look surprised. She told him he was projecting anxieties about his family onto the house because he couldn't deal with feeling trapped by them. What he couldn't deal with was psychiatry.

His mother said, "How does it feel to be back? I wasn't sure if I would ever see you again."

How did he feel? Free as a baby in his mother's arms.

The hallway was dotted with framed photos of the family, mostly without Alek. His father's retirement from the newspaper; Ben and Janelle with a pimpled Ivan at a barbecue; Giordana in cap and gown, with Jonah mock-kneeling like a supplicant next to her; Sasha and Damon in suits, dancing together at a party; Ruth and his mother, in sundresses and arm in arm, kicking, in a two-woman chorus line. The lone photo of Alek was so old it had a white border. The four of them at the beach, smiling for the camera. Teenaged Alek looking off to the side, one foot braced behind him in the sand, ready to jet out of the shot.

There was a mild risk to it, but he rearranged the frames, adding a few pictures of himself from over the years, not that he'd ever taken any. A small gesture, but it was finite. It felt right. Alek grinning at the grill in some kitchen he was working in; leading that group towards the steaming volcano two days before it erupted; huddled under a yellow rain poncho at the foot of some glacial waterfall, backpack hump behind him; some group shots, him with friends and girlfriends from along the way, sitting down to meals, picking beans, asleep in a giant oak.

His father was on the phone. "He seems all right, considering."

The last time Alek and his mother were in this hallway, they'd had a fight about medications.

Being new meant that he lived too long in his childhood bedroom, which came with its own difficulties. One of these was appearing normal. Unfortunately, his many attempts to stick to acceptable conversation and commonly understood timelines had failed. They could tell he was still a shade too playful with reality for an adult, which always led back to a doctor's office.

The first pills hadn't cured him, so they tried others. When those didn't work, they upped the dose, combining them with another family of pharmaceuticals, and then they hyphenated his diagnosis so it would all be justifiable.

What he received were side effects – shaking, thoughts that went nowhere, and a dead sex drive which translated into a dead everything. The ahistorical comments, though, hadn't slowed down a bit.

It was too much. The struggle to contain it all was turning him into a parody of what they wanted. At the next deadlock, he tried the big bluff: he admitted that he had made everything up. He promised he wouldn't do it anymore.

The excuse was as much a way out for him as it was for them. He would restrain himself from making further adjustments so there would be no more jumps in the record; they could pretend it was all a bad dream.

They didn't buy it. It was like blaming his disappearances on congestion. They accused him of pouching pills in his cheeks.

His father came up with a bargain: Alek could continue to live with them as long as they watched him swallow three different pills every night. That would be a condition of the comforts of home. Alternately, he could leave. There was no choice. If he stayed, he would become the drugged son in the upstairs bedroom.

Alek bounced his pack down the stairs towards the front door. His mother said, "Why don't you try what your father suggests for a few weeks."

His father followed close behind, knowing he wouldn't. "That's good, leave. You'll see. The first boss that doesn't think that showing up for work is optional, the first girl who doesn't want to smoke the same things that you smoke, we'll find out how strong your principles are then."

As he headed for the door, the three of them pushed through the narrow hall, crowding the space where he and his mother were currently standing. Alek wondered if she felt those people too.

After he had left that day, he stood on the top step like a man on a plank. If he waited long enough, she would come out and wave him back in. She didn't.

There was another angle to try before giving up. He went back a decade, to their first friction, the time when the routine of the house and high school were starting to get in the way of his exploration. He gave his mother a flex of sudden nerve and muscle. He couldn't go back and change himself, but he could change her. She would spy on him and discover his secrets. She would pin him down and make him talk. He would tell her. From there, they would have figured out a way to all live together. A change would come that would bring him back inside or send him with confidence into the world. Alek waited, but nothing happened. The new memories came to him. She had taken her strength in the wrong direction and Alek hadn't confided in her or anyone. Nothing was different. He was still standing out there alone with the front door he had slammed behind him. Just because it was magic didn't mean it was easy.

With Alek's additions, the photo wall had become much more welcoming, but he had been careless. If there were photos in the hall, there would have been letters. Brief, yes, but it meant contact when there had been almost none. He would have to ride this through, trying to keep a grip on the shape of the day. Already, these modifications had transformed his mood. The impulse to undo what he had done was gone.

Even the eagerness of the need in his mother's touch – it eased by a fraction.

"Everything is more or less where it's always been," she said, pushing away from him with a poke in his chest, "except where Dad and I have become too wizened to bend down or reach up." She turned her back to him. "You look well," she said, bracing herself against the wooden skirting with her fingertips. "Older, but that is apparently the only way we acquire all this alleged wisdom. I, for one, haven't attained enlightenment. Yet." A weak chuckle followed, while she moved gingerly down the hallway towards the kitchen.

As she walked, Alek noticed that the wall was still filling with pictures. They were scuffing the new paint job as they straightened themselves into rows. He had written to his parents, often, always with new photos. *Here I am arriving in another strange place. Here I am leaving it. Here I am full of resolve. Here I am full of resolve again.* They probably wrote two for every one of his.

Even though he could think back and remember months and years with no contact, the letters settled into him too. The tracks of his wanderings turned, if only to make sure he received the mail, wherever he was. The hundred letters he had received were treasured. They were a talisman of home. He became aware that every one of them was right there with him, cramming into a big manila folder at the top of his pack.

His father called from the kitchen, "There's cider in here if you want. We bought that brand you like."

The wall continued to change. A few of the friendly faces he had met along the way began to bleach away, leaving him on his own in a tent or at a beach. They would stay in his memory, but that was it. Their lives would have clicked into different plots. The shared meals, the muddy walks in inescapable rain – gone. Their memories of him would be getting scratched out right now.

The appearance of pictures slowed as the folder in his pack grew tight. All this new history took hold. Alek realised that he was comfy.

His bedroom had become his mother's studio. On top of the desk lay a recent painting of hers, a view of their garden from a grasshopper's height. There were no signs that he had lived here recently, which was a relief.

Still, remnants of his childhood and adulthood peeked at him from various corners. Two rows of sci-fi novels crammed together on the bottom of the bookshelf; the wooden peg-board game he'd made with his father, now a paperweight; the elephant print tucked behind the desk and sitting on the floor. The book he was after, *Tales from Other Lands,* was in a box marked 'Boys', high up on a wardrobe shelf. He opened to the last story to look at the illustration. It was as he re-membered it. A tan collage of a square-faced boy talking to a bright red swirl that took up most of the page. The image had imprinted on him, but he had forgotten the story:

There was once a boy who was too curious for his own good. He left his family's farm to make his fortune. Before he had even said his farewell to the dog – right outside the front gate – he met a giant snake. Its scales were the colour of rubies, and the snake said to him, "You must go back to your family." The boy said, "But I want to see the world." The snake said, "Their blood is your blood. They are yours, you are theirs, forever." The boy went back home and grew responsible. No one found out that he had even dreamed of seeing mountains and oceans. He helped his father with the animals and the fences. He worked with his mother to keep the garden and cook their meals. Occasionally he would write a goodbye note and pack some clothes and a bunch of carrots, but as soon as he'd leave, guess who would always be waiting for him? The snake spoke to him the same way every time. And every time the boy was back home before his note was ever found. Eventually, he fell in love with a woman from a nearby town and they built a house right next to his parents'. They married and had five children. They worked very hard, and were soon able to buy their own cows, pigs and chickens. They planted the best crops for the land they had and kept them productive year after year. The man and woman were happy much of the time, but they had to work long hours to keep everyone fed, especially when his parents grew frail. Thoughts of leaving were nearly forgotten. Whenever he had a fleeting idea of running away from his ever-increasing responsibilities, the snake would appear to him, sometimes in his own bed as he was falling asleep. "Their blood is your blood. They are yours and you are theirs, forever." His children grew up and fell in love. They left home to see mountains and oceans. No snake is stopping them, he thought to himself as each one of them went off. The boy became an old man, burying his father, his mother, and finally his wife, at the very back of the farm. Years later, when his breathing was difficult and his legs were shaky, he sold his livestock to a neighbour, packed the few possessions that mattered to him and started down the road. Immediately, the snake was there beside him. Before it could even speak, the man shouted, "What do you want? There's nobody left at home! There's no kin there to share a meal with me. Surely I can go to see what I've missed by staying here."

The snake raised its head high over the old man and said, "You have already seen all that this life has to offer you," and plunged his fangs through his shirt and into his heart. For an instant, the old man was enraged, his mouth opening and closing with injustice and blood. He had done what the snake had told him to do and this was his repayment! Staggering back against the fence that had given shape to his life, he looked into the snake's shining eyes and saw compassion. "The snake has protected me for all these years," was the last thought he had as he fell to the ground.

Endings could be so cruel. What was a child supposed to learn from that, except that you had to help your parents with chores? Alek was angry. He saw his six-year-old self on the carpet, lying on his stomach and staring down at the picture, trying to understand. He would have talked back to the picture, telling the snake to mind its own damned business and telling the boy to run as far as he could.

Once, on his own quest to see mountains and oceans, Alek had hooked up for a while with a relief worker when she was bouncing between gigs. She had been with a lot of flakes before, so she was onto him early. Too wild-eyed when he talked, no romantic past. She didn't know what she was after either, but all she knew was that one day he was going to get weird on her. Waiting till he was at ease, when his head was resting in her lap, she leaned forwards to find out what he was about. Her hair made a shimmering curtain around his face. They were alone. She made her move. "Quick: which word makes you feel better, 'tightrope' or 'net'?"

"Both," he said. It won him a very decent kiss, for honesty, if he remembered correctly. But she later used it as evidence that he would never be comfortable holding still with her.

By now, it was almost certain that they had never met.

Listening to the house he could still hear pictures skittering on the wall. This was not how the visit was supposed to go. He was choosing the net. Or the net was choosing him. He couldn't say for sure if it mattered anymore. Since Giordana had called, had he ever had a choice? In another hour this would be his bedroom again.

Alek and his father were out on the screened verandah saying little, when the caravan drove up. In one car, there was Ruth with Giordana and Jonah and their dog; in another, Sasha and Damon in the front, with Ben, Janelle and Ivan squished into the back.

They all spilled out. Jonah took Ruth's hand to lead her up the steps. Giordana retrieved a foil brick, Ruth's orange cake, from the car.

Ben and Ivan hung back, like they'd been forced to dress up and behave for the day, but Janelle leapt ahead, grinning at Alek as she took the five steps all at once, the way she used to. Ivan had become the tallest.

The dog was the one who beat them all to the front door and sat there, tail wagging with anticipation.

Alek followed Peter into the hallway, bracing himself for the full immersion.

Though he had visited each of them in recent years, he watched the way they saw him. Their caution and indulgence told him who he was: a grizzled man, shorter and less sparkly than he had once been. He had worn out the patience of a perfectly honest family and was still being given a hero's welcome.

Sasha pulled his brother into a buddy embrace, savouring it. Inevitably, he also forced a laugh at the importance of the moment, saying, "Wonderful, wonderful," in a precise imitation of their father.

Ben shook Alek's hand, but kept his distance, saying "You look well," and nothing else.

Janelle wrapped herself around Alek and clasped her hands tightly behind him. "I can't believe it's you. You were my first job!"

Ivan shook Alek's hand the same way his father did – uninterested in making an impression. He watched Alek with an uneasy smile, like he was sniffing around for schizophrenia.

"Do you even remember me?" Alek asked him.

"Barely," he said, startled, as if he hadn't expected Alek to speak.

Giordana pulled Alek close, till they were forehead to forehead. She gripped his shoulders with her usual intensity and said, "You feel so very good. Thank you."

From behind her, Jonah started to offer his greeting, but Ruth pushed through to plough her fingers through Alek's hair and cover his cheeks with kisses.

"There's some silver coming in around the edges, but we'll allow it," she said. She held him tight, so she wouldn't lose him again.

Remember: they're not asking you for a thing.

Ruth turned Alek's chin towards her, holding it under the hallway light so she could look at him. "Tell me. Do you have any stories for us, my sweet?"

Alek evaded the question with a smile.

The man he had sat next to on the plane saw him more clearly than she did. He was a house painter who lived six months of the year with his wife and travelled on his own for the other six. His wife was content to stay at home. "You'd think all that separate time, her at home and me getting myself lost, would lead to friction. Seventeen years says it doesn't. I come through the door and it's like any other Friday night."

Alek told the man believable bits of his own story. He found himself envying the man's wandering as well as the fact of his wife. Alek had never managed any balance. The wandering had become half-hearted – a juggling act he could sustain for no particular benefit; and the wife, well, she had never materialised. The man claimed to be jealous of Alek. He was being polite. Alek listened. The fond regard covered for what the man really saw: a vagabond mess. Their talk ran down after that, but as they parted at the baggage claim area, the man squeezed Alek's shoulder like they were old friends, "And what's next for you? What are you going to conjure up to make your family forgive you for abandoning them?"

Jonah pointed to the dog. "And this is Lance."

The collie was on all fours, groomed and proper. Alek squatted to greet him. Lance sniffed with minor interest. It was almost hurtful. Usually, animals were hypnotised by his fragrance and attention.

Giordana said, "Lance can be a bit circumspect at first."

That's dumb, Alek thought, and in a flash made himself familiar to the dog. Amazed at his own good fortune, Lance's eyes went big with excitement. A tap on the knee and he jumped up, licking madly. Alek scratched the dog's neck, and Lance fell against him in canine ecstasy. There, that was better.

As he stood up, Ben leaned in close, clapping a hand against Alek's shoulder, saying, "Ivan really appreciates you being here for this. Give him some of your time today, if you can. He talks about you for months after every visit."

Every visit? What would Lance have needed to get comfortable? Alek looked in the hall. More pictures were blinking open into new existence. There he was at graduations and barbecues at the pond. The memories would be seeping in shortly.

Janelle said, "Personally, I think you provided him with the spark to take a risk like this."

Alek took a step away from the family circle. It was safer to observe what else was different before saying something foolish. He reverted to his silent self. A few pictures shuffled themselves on the wall. Only Alek saw.

Once, he had tried to demonstrate this shift to Vicenta, hoping that her hawk-eyed attention would catch it midstream. Protesting the absurdity of the whole thing, she agreed to write down her wish on a piece of paper. It was for a pair of grey ankle boots that she could in no way afford. Easy. Making her keep her eyes focused, Alek put the boots on her feet. She was dumbfounded. In the instant after that, the other details followed and she was furious that he had taken her mother's money to buy them. This was before he had mastered any delicacy. "You can't always get what you want," he started to sing, but she wasn't amused. In another few seconds, the piece of paper in her hand disappeared, as did the thrill of her new boots.

"What?" she said to him, exasperated. It was like he was alone.

"Nice boots," he said.

"Don't change the subject."

The subject of the day, it turned out, was Ivan's big trip. Alek had been visiting, but everyone had come for Ivan's going away party. Peter had cooked all morning and they would have a late lunch before sending him off to the airport. Ivan was the one collecting all the hugs and questions. And Alek was the one responsible for Ivan's wanderlust. The tinkering had been worthwhile. His visits home had yielded a result more impressive than a responsive dog.

At lunch, Ben talked a lot about carbon footprints while the others copped to various wasteful behaviour.

Alek decided to listen instead.

Giordana wanted Ruth to buy a safer car, but there was nothing she could tell her mother that wouldn't result in Ruth whipping out a stapled journal article to prove exactly why Giordana wasn't fully informed.

Jonah watched his wife eat salad, experiencing what he could only describe as 'a certain thrill'. Since she'd gone vegetarian, there had been a distinct uptick in her sex drive.

Ben was sorry that his son was taking this big life adventure by himself. When Ben and Janelle did their travelling, they had their send-off right in this room, with Janelle's parents still alive. It was romantic, like a pre-wedding honeymoon. Going it alone was so – solitary.

Janelle wondered why she was wasting precious brain space on a flirtation with a work colleague. He was married and lived one time zone away. Still, he would be working at her office for the next two months. She would be tempted. Nothing would ever happen, or if it did, it would lead directly to trouble. Maybe all she wanted was the drama. She looked around at everyone and wondered if she could find the nerve to leave them.

Sasha had the brochures with him for the place he wanted his parents to move to. It was closer to the city. It was co-housing, all ages, so they wouldn't feel like they'd been dumped with a lot of other seniors. No stairs. The garden was shared. How could they say no?

Damon hadn't told Sasha about the layoffs coming at his office. He wasn't definitely out but he wasn't definitely in. Better to mention it now. Maybe later in the car. If he and Sasha could get a better mortgage nailed down while he still had his job, they could keep everything swinging.

Ruth was irritated with the dimness of the women in her book group. If she was going to make good on her threat to quit, she wanted to have a better activity lined up. She had no clue what it would be. With Ivan gone, she'd see Ben less than ever, so there'd be even more time for clients, but they were wearing her out. If Giordana would allow it, they could plan a once-a-week phone call for half an hour that would be a dedicated book group for just the two of them. Ruth would be willing to read from Giordana's area of study, if that was what she wanted. Never in a million billion years would her daughter say yes to a plan like that.

Alek's father was going over the Skype instructions Ivan had given him. As if this would make up for the distance while he was away. Ivan's visits had been a bottomless cup and now he was leaving them. Not one of the kids gave a second thought to jumping on a plane and flying away. But Ivan should enjoy himself. Peter hoped that whenever Ivan settled down he had a bunch of kids, if only to keep the family's numbers up. A pack of them, so they would protect each other and remember Ivan after he was gone. Tomorrow, Alek's father wanted to clear out the kitchen cabinets to figure out exactly where the mice were getting in.

After lunch, Alek's mother was going to ask Ruth to come live with them. She could take Alek's room. It wasn't for her old nursing skills, though they would inevitably come in handy. It was more emotional than that. She wasn't embarrassed to voice it: she wanted her little sister closer. In fact, she wanted everyone closer. Constantly. As close as they were right now. Looking at the faces at the table, she could eat all of them up, as her grandmother used to say. That way she would always know where they were. They would be inside her, always.

Ivan was thinking about the books he had packed for his trip. Over lunch, he decided to leave them in Alek's room. Plus, the iPod and camera. They were all middle-men for the experiences he would have. A few changes of clothes and an ATM card would do it. He couldn't wait to get away. Additionally, he was planning to masturbate on the plane.

Alek felt no need for any intervention. Mostly, they had managed this long without him. They would continue.

"You have that elsewhere look in your face," Giordana whispered to Alek. "Do you want to take a walk around the block?"

"No," Alek said. "It's strange. I like it here."

"It's not that strange," she said.

To his surprise, the person he understood most at the table was his mother. All the faces, with the hundred-armed clatter simmering behind them, this was what he'd been missing. They were his and he was theirs.

Alek surveyed the house, not sure where he belonged. Ivan gave him a wink from the kitchen doorway and asked for one last game of basketball before he had to head to the airport. Apparently, Alek had also learned how to play basketball.

In the living room, Sasha was spreading out the brochures while his father scoured the room for his reading glasses.

"Really," Sasha called out to Alek in the hall, "you might like the vibe of this community." Alek held up his palm. No thanks.

"They've got places for crazy bachelors like yourself." Sasha said.

Their father shook his head at Sasha. "You're a cut-up. Leave him be."

Directly under the hall light, Giordana held Natalie's head at an angle so a few stray whiskers could be trimmed from her cheek. Janelle was showing off her new phone to both of them. His mother waved at him with her right hand and said, "Beauty treatment."

Alek called to her, "You wanted to leave a message for the physio."

She was perplexed. "About what?"

"To reschedule. You mentioned it when we were coming in before."

"From where?"

The conversation hadn't happened.

"Never mind. I misremembered."

She gave a furrowed glance to Giordana. Right. If he

planned to stick around, he would have to stay silent. Otherwise, the cycle of specialists would begin again.

He looked at the pictures on the wall. Where had he been for the last decade: here or travelling?

Ivan was still in the doorway, spinning the basketball on the tip of his forefinger. "What's up, Al? Are you in or are you out?"

Ben gave Alek a friendly shove. "Don't take all afternoon to ponder it. Go give the kid one game. We don't have him around for long."

In front of the garage, Alek's fingers grazed the ball on its way up and he missed the shot.

Ivan grabbed it, drove it up the driveway and dunked it. He softened his win with a confession. "The real deal is, I'm kind of nervous about the trip."

"That's healthy. It'll keep you alert. Lots of freaks out there. Freaks who want things."

"That's not what you're supposed to be telling me." He kept possession and made another easy shot. "Can't you paint some beautiful lie about how cool it's going to be?"

Alek picked up the ball. "It's not. Not all the time."

"Fucking nifty. But that's true if I stay home, too."

"True," Alek said. "Anything can happen, anywhere. You can be flying over your neighbour's house and looking in the windows, or you can be dying on your bed upstairs. Or you can be playing your very first game of basketball right this very minute." Alek tried to emphasise his point with a basket, but missed.

"What?"

At least he hadn't lost his ability to confuse. Ivan stole the ball and Alek chased him up and down the driveway, already puffing. "All I mean is there's no profit in worrying. By the time you get where you're going, the story will have changed anyway."

"Easy to say," Ivan dunked again. He finally took pity and passed to his uncle, who fumbled it.

Ivan looked doubtful. "You're way off today. Should we quit?"

The ball rolled behind the garage. Alek didn't see much reward in going after it.

"I think so. Tell me: what would help your trip? What do you want most of all?"

Ivan raised his eyebrows, looking for permission to wish big.

Alek nodded.

Ivan made a devilish smile as he went after the ball. Kicking his way through the hedge, he retrieved it. He bounced it against the side of the garage for a solid minute. On a final bounce, Ivan caught it and held it to his chest.

"It would be sweet if you were coming with me," he said.

Alek found Janelle and Ben in the backyard, standing with Giordana, Jonah and Peter, and watching Lance do minor tricks.

Jonah was selling them on a dog. "I'm not saying it would replace Ivan exactly, but they are more obedient."

Ben and Janelle gave half-hearted smiles.

Alek reported Ivan's request, casually, to see how the adults would take it.

With a straight face Janelle said, "Would you? A real adult, at least at the start of this expedition. I'd feel so much better if you were there."

Ben added, "And of course Ivan would adore it."

Giordana and Jonah thought it was a reasonable idea.

Even his father said, "Would you make sure he keeps himself showered and maybe even shaved?"

Alek had impressed them so much on these visits of his that he had graduated to trusted chaperone. "Will do."

"But Ivan's flying tonight," Janelle said.

"I've got a friend at the airport," Alek said, arranging his ticket even as they stood there.

Janelle said, "Please. This wasn't what you were planning to do today. Would you at least let us pay half?"

They were always uneasy if they didn't understand where his money came from. He made more sense if he was a sponge. "Sure."

Before heading back inside, temptation beat his resolve. He brushed past Ben and Janelle, touching them each on an elbow. He squeezed as if he was grateful for their approval, but also stunned them back to the day before they decided to get married. They looked alarmed, as if what they were feeling might be visible to others. They caught each other's glances.

There, that would give her some drama to work out.

Alek's bag was already packed, not because he had arrived that morning but because leaving with Ivan had always been the plan. His mother insisted that he take a fresh towel, meaning one of the green ones from his childhood. It was rough from years of sun, but he folded it into his pack next to the letters, like another treasure. Ruth wrapped up some sandwiches and a few slices of cake for the ride to the airport. Sasha forced phone cards into Ivan's hand. "They work anywhere except the moon."

The entire visit home had taken a few hours, but the goodbyes were easy. They lacked the shakiness of his arrival. No one but Alek remembered that anymore. A stream of his visits had filled in the missing years, so the embraces were ordinary. The only extra pull came from the usual place, the endless human hope that they would all live long enough to hug each other on another afternoon.

The plane half-rounded the airport and flung out into its arc over the ocean. As soon as the sparkle of buildings disappeared in a haze, Ivan stopped watching from the rounded window. He paged through the in-flight magazine, coming up with a schedule for all the movies he would watch.

"Doesn't it seem illegal, flying off like this?" he asked.

"Why?"

"What if my parents need me or something?"

"They survived before you showed up, they'll survive without you for a while."

"They're older though."

"They're not that old. They'll be all right. Your mother, I should tell you, is going to live to be one hundred. And healthy."

"How do you know that?"

"Because once, when she was your age, that was what she wanted."

"And she gets what she wants, doesn't she?" Ivan asked.

"As much as any of us."

The relief of departure inundated Ivan and he was asleep before the seatbelt light switched off. Alek reached across to slide down his shade. The sun had diffused to a band of colourless light across the horizon. They would be into daylight in a few hours.

Thoughts had been gathering together. All the alternate histories he remembered were adding up, organising themselves without his efforts – like the frames in the hall – into a single idea. He looked at Ivan's closed eyes and saw his parents and Ruth, all of them. They were the only people who couldn't forget he existed and here he was, flying off again.

No right thinking person would give up the abilities he had, but there had never been a right thinking person to ask. This was what his mother should have been crying about, but Alek allowed the thoughts to draw him further in.

The lights above the other seats in the cabin went off one by one. Imagine it: no wishes to grant, no confusion over what had changed. Alek rubbed his hands across his face. Even as he did it, he felt its source: it was his father's gesture of surrender.

No more trying to remember which stories were true. Other people's desires would be out of his jurisdiction. This was the freedom he'd needed. A single thought and it could be done.

This would be remembered as the moment of his undoing, no doubt. He would finally experience the same powerlessness as those around him. His family would struggle, but he wouldn't be able to save them. He would wake up to the first tick of his own death, but he wouldn't be able to do anything about it. Maybe he would find peace with a partner – but that

too would lead to suffering that he couldn't repair. The others would be by his side, consoling. *You did what you could.* He alone would know what he might have been able to do, what he had lost.

No, he could fix that too. There would be no more solitary slabs of memory. He could forget his powers.

"Water?" The stewardess held out a tray of half-filled cups.

"Thanks," Alek said, fitting one into the appointed groove on his tray table. A circle linked perfectly inside another. He pressed his thumb along the edge of the cup. It was half full. If they hit turbulence, it wouldn't even spill.

"It's a long flight. You tell me if there's anything I can do for you." She continued up the aisle with the same offer for everyone else.

The only light that was on was his.

Alek lifted the cup to his lips.

Acknowledgements

The Booranga Writers' Centre, Varuna, Rosebank Retreat and the Victorian Writers' Centre each provided me with time, support and places to work on this book. My fellow nurses at Eastern Palliative Care always gave me the roster I needed to continue living my double life as a writer. The Third Monday Writing Group and the Young & Jackson Writing Group were perceptive and generous readers. Sharon Block, Toni Jordan, Nelson Mathews, Peter Mendelsund, Jennifer Morgan and Nicola Redhouse brought their sharpness to early drafts. Then, at the exact right moment, Stuart Williams stepped in with his intelligence and sense (editorial and otherwise). Corry De Neef was, and is, wise and indulgent and wonderful. I am grateful to all.